SIX DAYS
IN JUNE

Other books by Judy Kouzel:

Her Lifelong Dream
A Dreamer's Romance

SIX DAYS IN JUNE

•

Judy Kouzel

AVALON BOOKS
NEW YORK

Published by Thomas Bouregy & Co., Inc.
160 Madison Avenue, New York, NY 10016

Library of Congress Cataloging-in-Publication Data

Kouzel, Judy.
  Six days in June / Judy Kouzel.
    p. cm.
  ISBN-13: 978-0-8034-9842-6 (acid-free paper)
  I. Title.
  PS3611.O7494S59 2007
  813'.6—dc22

                                    2007011963

PRINTED IN THE UNITED STATES OF AMERICA
ON ACID-FREE PAPER
BY HADDON CRAFTSMEN, BLOOMSBURG, PENNSYLVANIA

To Erin Cockey and Megan Rubino

Thanks to Erin, Faith, Susan, Bob and all the other great people at Avalon who help me at every turn. Also thanks to my husband, kids and insane sisters, who stubbornly remain standing in my corner.

Chapter One

Abigail Gibson, aka Abe, was frantically searching her bedroom for her lavender-dyed high heels. "Darn it," she said to her dog, Bailey. "Have you seen them? I left them right here . . . I think." Abe yanked open the door to her closet again and began pulling shoes out of the cubbies of the wooden shoe holder that had gone from being practical to inadequate in a matter of days. "Mom," she shouted. "Have you seen my lavender shoes?"

The silence was deafening, as Abe knew it would be. Her mother was quite firm in her opinions that grown women should know where their shoes were at all times. A theory that Abe couldn't argue with and one that she lived by, most of the time. She clearly remembered putting the shoes, box and all, on the top shelf in her closet. But then came the fittings for her maid-of-honor dress and each time, she brought the shoes along.

1

There had been some problems with the bodice of the dress, but today was the last of the fittings, hopefully.

Abe glanced at the floor and saw that things had once again become cluttered. She sighed and started arranging the mess at the bottom. That's when she saw the shoebox, right where she left it, sitting neatly in the corner on the floor. "There they are," Abe said, looking at Bailey with an accusing look. She then headed for the door, hoping against hope that the bride was running late too.

Megan Randal and Abe became friends on the first day of kindergarten when Megan stood behind Abe against the wall as they waited in line to get their snacks. Not one to waste time with formalities, Megan asked, "Will you be my best friend?"

"Yes," Abe answered after relatively little deliberation and sealed the deal by holding hands. And that's what they've been ever since, despite Megan's later confession that had Abe declined her offer of friendship she'd planned to kick her in the kneecap.

"Best Friend" was what they called each other, although now that they were both twenty-four the term was beginning to sound juvenile. Still, "Best Friend" was an applicable phrase, nonetheless. They attended the same elementary, middle, and high schools together, as well as the same summer camps, dance classes, soccer teams, and cheerleading squads. They'd even received their driver's licenses on the same day and double-dated on their senior prom. They both attended North Carolina State University together (Go Wolfpack!). Their mothers had long-ago accepted that the two girls were perfectly content to spend each and every day in each other's company and that separating them was pointless. Why fight it? It was Megan and Abe. Abe and Megan. The two went together like peanut butter and jelly.

Megan Randal was petite and curvy with long, shiny, thick brown hair that refused to curl no matter what she did. She wore it down her back or in a swinging ponytail or sometimes in a tousled, messy bun. She had flawless olive skin and big doe-like brown eyes. Years of cheerleading had given her a healthy, athletic body. She was cute and bouncy and had a booming, laughing voice. But her small stature and pretty face often led people to believe she was a sweet and even-tempered little thing—a myth she quickly shattered. As many good qualities as Megan had, she was far from sweet-tempered and demure. In fact, nothing could be further from the truth, and it never took anyone long to realize it.

Megan's mother called her "spunky," and her father called her "pigheaded" because of her flair for drama and her habit of saying the first thing that popped into her head. Her outspoken ways often landed her into deep trouble, although lately she was finally learning to think before she spoke.

Abe understood Megan better than anyone, except for possibly her future husband, Billy. Abe understood Megan's many moods almost as well as she understood her own. She knew that Megan was both spunky and pigheaded, and she liked her friend's multifaceted, energetic personality. Abe liked Megan.

Megan was a drama queen and a poet, a know-it-all

who bragged a lot but who was also a champion for the underdog. She was impatient and strong-willed, but she was also fiercely loyal to her family and friends. She loved being the center of attention but was always happy to share the spotlight with her friends. She loved to have fun and to laugh. She was independent and strong one minute, dark and intense the next. To Megan Randal, life was meant to be lived well. She was Abe's best friend for life.

Abe was pretty too, but as physically different from Megan as she could possibly be. She was tall where Megan was petite, and lanky where Megan was curvy. Her long, baby-fine hair was strawberry blond with soft waves, nothing like Megan's thick, straight mane of dark brown tresses. Abe's facial features were fine and delicate too. Her skin was as fair as fine porcelain, and her nose was narrow and perfect, with a spatter of freckles across the bridge. Her eyes were a stormy blue, and her cheeks seemed to be eternally kissed with a soft shade of pink. Her voice was lilting, and she spoke with a slow, easy accent that identified her as a North Carolina native. There was a flower petal softness to Abe—a china teacup-and-lace quality that made people approach her with care. That was, of course, until she threw back her head and gave one of her howling belly laughs, or slapped them on the back while telling one of her funny stories. Abe Gibson looked as if she was a fragile, delicate flower, but she wasn't.

Megan met Billy at an N.C. State football game almost eighteen months ago. Megan and Abe were there with a group of other school alumni, jumping up and down and screaming for their alma mater until their throats were hoarse. They shouted and cheered and behaved more like giddy freshmen than graduates, but they didn't care if they looked silly. They were there to have a good time. Billy Meegan was in the row ahead of them, studying the game with all the seriousness of a monk and occasionally looking over his shoulder at the raucous, noisy people behind him.

"Get a look at him," Susie Keating, Megan's new friend from work whispered. "He's cute, isn't he?"

"Too cute," Megan said, wrinkling her nose. "He looks like a teenager."

"I don't know," Susie said. "I think he's kind of hot. Don't stare. He's looking at me."

But Megan couldn't help but stare. Just one look at the young man in the row ahead of her gave her unexpected butterflies in her stomach. She tried to shake off this strange, new emotion, but then Billy looked over his shoulder at her and smiled. A lock of blond hair fell carelessly over his eyes, and Megan felt her knees go weak. Then she smiled back at him.

Billy Meegan was not too tall and not too short, which was perfect for Megan. He had a mop of blond hair and gray-blue eyes. There was a boyish quality to Billy that charmed Megan to her toes. A freckle-faced, pug-nosed cuteness she sensed he'd never outgrow. Of course this quality initially led Megan to believe she could wrap him around her little finger—something she'd easily done with all the boyfriends who came along before him. But Megan quickly learned that Billy wasn't going to be like her other boyfriends. She soon gave up on trying to control him and fell in love with him instead.

Abe was ecstatic when Billy proposed to Megan and wanted to be a part of every single detail, if only to ensure that Megan's wedding was everything she'd ever dreamed it would be. But then she realized she was virtually clueless as to what exactly was involved in planning a wedding. True, she'd been a bridesmaid in her fair share of friends' weddings, but that always seemed to be more fun and games than anything else. To Abe, weddings were an opportunity to wear a pretty dress and dance the night away. Sure there was some work to do; but with everyone doing their share, it was never overwhelming. Actually Abe was never particularly involved in the planning process before. But with Megan, she came along on all the shopping trips and joined her in poring over the bridal magazines looking for the "perfect" gown or the "perfect" color theme for the reception. Together they planned all the necessary requirements down to the last detail. Thinking of all the minutiae that was involved made Abe's head spin. She'd naively thought that a wedding was merely a gathering of family and friends to witness a couple take the vows of holy matrimony. She never knew about the horrendous amount of work that occurred behind the scenes. But, then again, Abe was unlike many young women in that she never gave much thought to weddings. As a child, she'd never once dressed up in a long, white dress and pretended to walk down an imaginary aisle. Nor had she once purchased a bridal magazine "just for fun." The truth of the matter was that Abe didn't really care about such things. She'd always assumed that when the time came for her own wedding, she'd handle it like she handled everything else in her life—she'd throw herself full force on top of it and wrestle it into submission until it became exactly what she wanted. In short, Abe hadn't given weddings much thought until her best friend became engaged.

There were so many decisions to make. Decisions Abe never knew existed. There was the gown and the flowers, of course, but there was also the wedding vows (traditional or original?), the music (band or DJ?), the lineup of bridesmaids and groomsmen (every one should "match," and it was preferable that they didn't despise each other), not to mention the reception hall and the menu (sit-down or buffet?). The decision-making was never ending, and it seemed as if no detail was too small or too trivial. Every aspect was considered and given the same importance as one would give to planning the coronation of a queen. Abe was shocked by the amount of work involved in planning Megan's wedding, and she sometimes wondered if it was worth all the fuss. After all, wouldn't a trip to the justice of the peace produce the same result? But, then again, this was Megan's wedding. And the level of fuss was hers to decide on. Abe was not only determined to be a world class maid of honor, but to also do everything in her power to see to it that Megan's wedding was everything she dreamed it would be.

Chapter Two

"Do you realize that in four short weeks, your name is going to be Megan Meegan?" Abe said grinning from behind the large lunch menu in front of her.

"Don't remind me," Megan said, rolling her big chocolate-brown eyes and giving Abe a look of warning.

"Four weeks, Meg!"

"I remember. June 23rd, right?"

"That's the date. Will you be busy that day?"

"Very."

It was a beautiful warm day in Raleigh, North Carolina, and it was the first time in weeks the two friends had seen each other. The final fitting had gone as smooth as glass but had afforded them little chance to talk. Lunch at Magnolia's was the first opportunity Megan and Abe had to sit down together and catch up on each other's lives—it was also a good opportunity for Abe to tease the bride-to-be.

"You could always use your given name," Abe suggested, buttering the roll she'd taken from the basket the waiter brought them. "It so becomes you."

"You know I hate when people call me Gwendolyn," Megan shot back. "I much prefer to use my second middle name. I don't know what my mother was thinking anyway."

"Your mother named you after your two grandmas, remember?"

"She should have asked me first," Megan grumbled. The conversation brought up the old joke between Megan and her mother. Mrs. Randal had named her youngest child Gwendolyn Francine Megan Randal, a moniker which her daughter detested. And Megan never let an opportunity pass to poke fun at her mother's choice in names. "Everyone's called me Megan from the moment I came home from the hospital," she said often. "No one ever called me Gwendolyn! Or Francine!"

"I don't know," Abe said. "I kind of like the name Gwendolyn. It's pretty."

"Yuck!"

"Or Franny. That's a cute name."

"Quit teasing," Megan said, keeping the game going. "I could get even, you know."

Abe smiled. "Oh, yeah?"

"Yeah, *Abigail.*"

Abe winced. "Abigail is *my* grandma's name," she said, tartly. "My friends call me Abe . . . and you've made your point."

"Good," Megan said. "Now what are you having for lunch? I'm starved."

"I think I'll have the club sandwich. How about you?"

"That sounds good. I'm going to have the potato soup and a salad." After the waiter came and they ordered their food, Megan said cautiously, "You know, Abe, now that you bring up the subject of names, there's something I've been meaning to ask you."

"What's that?" Abe asked, taking another sip of sweet tea.

"This comes by special request from my mother . . . so, don't get mad, okay?"

"Uh-oh. This doesn't sound good."

"Oh, it's no big deal really. It's just that she says she wants you to go by your given name for the wedding."

"Your mother wants to call me . . . Abigail?"

"Yes, but it's just until after the wedding, of course." Megan rolled her eyes again, letting Abe know that she thought the request was silly. "Don't take it personally, Abe. She wants Susie to go by Susan."

"How come?" Abe asked, frowning. "Doesn't she like my name?"

"Yes. Of course she does. It's just that she prefers that you use your given name during the wedding events."

"Oh?"

"It's just for the wedding stuff though. After that you can go back to being Abe. She wants everything to be very formal. You know how my mother is."

Abe knew exactly how Megan's mother was. She'd known Mrs. Randal for as long as she'd known Megan and loved her dearly. She'd always been a wonderful lady, a bit too prim and proper when it came to social niceties, but a wonderful lady all the same. And a great mom, despite the Gwendolyn Francine Megan incident. But she was also Linda Randal, wife of the Honorable Judge Hank Randal and, as such, it was her job to make sure her family was always presented in the most respectable, upstanding, virtuous light possible. And it was a job Linda Randal took seriously.

"That's my mom," Megan said, with her ponytail bobbing away. "She's afraid my father's hoity-toity business associates and our relatives from New York will get the wrong idea. What would they think if they knew I have friends named Abe and Susie in my wedding? The scandal would rock the very foundation of Raleigh, wouldn't it?" Megan's voice was getting louder, as it often did when she wanted to make a point.

"Don't you think you're being a bit dramatic?"

"Yes," Megan said, sweeping her arms wide and knocking over the pepper shaker. "I'm being extremely dramatic but it's only because of my mother. Personally, I don't care if you and Susie call yourselves Fred One and Fred Two. All I care about is that my wedding day is perfect in every way. Unfortunately, my mother has a narrower view of what constitutes a perfect wedding. I'm sorry."

"Hmpf," Abe said, studying Megan's anxious face. "I've never realized how stressful weddings are until you became engaged, Meg. There are so many people you have to try and make happy. And all along I've been thinking that you'd become a bridezilla!"

"I am a bridezilla," Megan snapped. "And don't you forget it either! But my mother is an even bigger bridezilla!"

"Really?"

"It's sad but true, Abe, but when it comes to my wedding, I find it's best if I do exactly what my mother tells me. I have to pick my battles carefully."

"That's probably a good plan, but my name's Abe. Not Abigail."

"I know. Personally, I think Abe is a nice name, but you know my mom. And it isn't that she doesn't like your name or that she wishes you'd change it. Even if she could do that, she wouldn't. You're Abe always and forever. It's just that my mother wants my wedding to be a formal affair. I'm lucky she isn't making me go by Gwendolyn Francine. Besides, it's just for the wedding events—not for when you and I are out shopping or just hanging out. The only time we have to call you Abigail is when we're out with the other members of the wedding party. The rest of the time, you can go back to being Abe, like always."

"You mean for the reception and the rehearsal dinner?"

"Yeah, and the cookout. All the pre-wedding parties where we'll all be there together."

Abe opened her mouth to argue but decided against it because of the pleading look on Megan's face. Abe knew Mrs. Randal was becoming increasingly psychotic over the past few weeks due to the wedding preparations. She'd go from doting, warm and affectionate one minute to grouchy and unreasonable the next. Then she'd turn back again. It was clear that the pressure of the wedding had taken hold of the Randal household, and it wasn't going to let go until the very last drop of Champagne was gone. Abe saw Megan's anxious expression and thought that maybe her friend was feeling the strain a little too much.

"All right," Abe said. "I'll be Abigail . . . but only when we're with the wedding party and only until the wedding. After that I'm Abe again."

"It's a deal."

"And you owe me. You have to do whatever I want from now on."

"Wait a minute! No way. You're going to make me eat worms or something."

"No I'm not," Abe smiled because she couldn't imagine such a thing. "But I do get to tease you about your name being Megan Meegan."

"Must you?" Megan sighed.

"Yes."

"Even though you know I will exact a horrible revenge."

"Yes."

"I did mention the revenge would be horrible, didn't I?"

"Yep," Abe said. "And I'm duly terrified—but it's worth it."

Megan sighed again. "Very well. Don't say I didn't warn you."

"Does your mom want Billy to go by William?" Abe asked.

"Ha!" Megan said. "She tried but Billy wouldn't

hear of it. Even my mother's powers of intimidation have their limits."

Abe smiled. *Good for Billy,* she thought to herself.

Abe liked Billy Meegan and had known right away that he was the one for Megan. There was something about the way they looked at each other and about the way that they were instantly a couple. It was almost as if they'd been waiting for each other all along. Even now almost two years later, Billy and Megan were still madly, passionately in love.

"How did your dress fit?" Megan asked.

"Great," Abe said. "It's a beautiful gown. I love it!"

"It is pretty, isn't it?" Megan said, her eyes sparkling. "And, don't worry. I'm sure you'll wear it again." Megan threw her head back for a long, maniacal laugh, and Abe joined in with equal malevolence. The truth of that statement was clear to both of them. Over the past three years, they'd each collected an impressive array of bridesmaid dresses, none of which were ever worn again.

"I was thinking of wearing the pink slinky one from Molly's wedding to your rehearsal dinner," Abe said.

"The one that's cut down to your belly button?"

"That's the one."

"Over my mother's dead body! I don't know what Molly was thinking with that little number. She's usually more funky than sleazy."

"I don't know either. I think some sales lady got hold of her in a moment of weakness. Either that or one of the bridesmaids insisted we all wanted it. But I'll get my four hundred dollars out of it—even if it means I have to wear it to church on Easter."

"Well, you could wear it on a date," Megan said sweetly. Too sweetly. Abe's internal alarm bell began to ring frantically.

"No thanks," she said. "I was thinking of donating all of my dresses to the high school to use at their prom dress swap night. Maybe some teenager can wear a turtleneck underneath and . . ."

"Speaking of dates . . ."

"We weren't speaking of dates, Meg. No one was speaking of dates."

"Well, we could be speaking of dates."

"We could, but we won't."

"Oh, come on, Abe," Megan crooned. "If you don't have a date for Saturday night, Billy has this friend you'd flip for. He's—"

"Stop right there!" Abe said. "I thought we agreed the last time we had this conversation, I don't want any more blind dates! You promised that you and Billy wouldn't try to fix me up again, Meg."

"We agreed that I wouldn't set you up on any more blind dates with people I hadn't pre-approved. I've met this one, and he's completely different. He's an old friend of Billy's from high school who just moved back to town. They've known each other forever. He's going to be the best man. Coincidentally, he'll be the one who will walk you back down the aisle after the ceremony. I like him, Abe. He's the sweetest, nicest guy you could ever hope to meet."

"That's what you said about the guy who wore a Hawaiian shirt every day of his life. Remember, the one who kept talking about keggers?"

"You mean Chad?" Megan grimaced.

"Yes, I mean Chad! Or should I say Mad Chad? That's what he wanted me to call him."

"I told Billy that Chad wouldn't work out. He's much too juvenile for you."

"And what about Bobby? Remember Bobby? He was the one that said 'ya know what I mean?' after every sentence. The trouble is, Megan, I never knew what he was saying."

"That's not fair, Abe. Bobby's working hard to improve his communication skills. He's come a long way over the past six months."

"And how about the guy who let it slip that he was out on parole? What was his name? Brett?"

"It was his first offense!" Megan exclaimed. "Everyone deserves a second chance, right?"

"Yuck!" Abe said. "He was creepy!"

"I know," Megan winced. "I'm sorry about that one, Abe. Really I am. Billy's mother invited Brett's family over for a cookout after they moved in across the street. How was Billy supposed to know that Brett was an ex-convict? He seemed like a nice guy at first."

"He finally stopped calling last month."

"I'm sorry about Brett, Abe, but this guy is different. I promise! Except for—"

"No. Besides, I've already made plans for this weekend. We're supposed to meet everyone at the restaurant Saturday night, remember? Let's just leave it at that."

Abe shuddered at the thought of yet another blind date orchestrated by Megan and Billy. So far, she'd gone on four blind dates with "great guys" she had absolutely nothing in common with. After the Brett fiasco, Abe told Megan her blind date days were over. That was three months ago, and Megan hadn't brought up the subject since then. Until now.

"Come on, Abe."

"No!" she said again. "Don't you have more important things to do one month before your wedding than play matchmaker?"

"Even if I got you tickets to see Refreshments in the Lobby?"

"You got tickets to see Refreshments in the Lobby?" Abe gaped at her, stunned. Refreshments in the Lobby was her favorite band of all time. They played a mix of country and rock 'n' roll—the type of music that was suddenly being called alternative country. Abe had loved Refreshments in the Lobby ever since their debut album, before anyone else had heard of them and before they'd become megastars. Before tickets had become almost impossible to buy at any price. The news that Megan had somehow gotten tickets to their show was enough to take Abe's breath away. "How'd you get them?" she gasped.

"I didn't," Megan said. "But I tried to! They were sold out in the first hour. I went online as soon as they went on sale, but my computer crashed."

"I know," Abe said. "I tried to get tickets too. But how would you have been able to go? That concert is a one-day show, and it's the day after your wedding. You'll be on your honeymoon then."

"I know," Megan said. "I was going to surprise you with the tickets as a gift. I know how much you love Refreshments in the Lobby."

"That's sweet of you."

"It is, isn't it?"

"Thanks."

"You're welcome. If I'd gotten the tickets it would have been perfect. You could have gone with Jack."

"Who's Jack? I would have probably picked Kasey or Taylor or Chandler to go since I don't know anyone named Jack."

"Then you wouldn't have been able to get the tickets. There's a catch to getting free tickets."

"There is?"

"Yes. Jack would have had to go with you. You would have gone together. He likes Refreshments in the Lobby too, I think."

"I wouldn't have gone then."

"Not even to see Refreshments in the Lobby?"

"I don't know," Abe said thoughtfully. "Maybe. What difference does it make? The concert tickets sold out fast, and neither one of us was able to get any tickets."

"You should meet Jack anyway," Megan said. "He's good-looking and nice and has a great sense of humor. You'd really like him, Abe, except for his—"

"Sorry," Abe interrupted. "Thanks, Megan, but no thanks. I've had enough blind dates to last a lifetime. I'm all done with them so, please, please, pretty please, no more matchmaking!"

"But . . ."

"No buts," Abe said firmly.

"Oh, all right, but . . ."

"I said no buts."

"Okay," Megan said, reluctantly. "I was just going to tell you that he's hot. And a great guy too! And he's nice! He's a hot, great, nice guy. I'd nab him myself if I hadn't already met my dreamboat."

"Megan," Abe groaned. "I know you're in love with Billy, but that doesn't mean I have to fall in love with one of his friends, does it?"

"Yes," Megan said. "We've talked about this before, remember? You and I are best friends. It only stands to reason that the men we fall in love with will be best friends. That way we can all be best friends forever. Then we'll get married and move into pretty houses right next door to each other. And then we'll both have adorable little babies—probably within a few minutes of each other. Then they'll be best friends too! Isn't that the way we always planned it?"

Abe smiled, remembering their carefully laid plans from childhood. "Megan Meegan," she said, shaking her head. "You're hopeless."

"I know," she said. "But I'm just reminding you of the plan. And stop calling me Megan Meegan. You promised!"

"I'll make you a deal," Abe said. "But the offer is only good for the next three minutes."

"What's that?"

"I won't call you Megan Meegan as long as you don't set me up on any more blind dates."

"Don't you want a date for the wedding?" Megan knew she was asking a loaded question, but she asked it anyway.

"No, not particularly," Abe said, wrinkling her nose. "I don't have any interest whatsoever in going to your wedding with a date because a) I'm going to be too busy with my maid-of-honor duties to pay any attention to him, and b) I don't need to be on a date with some bozo you set me up with to enjoy myself."

"I agree with you," Megan said, "in theory, but I know if you met Jack you'd flip for him. And that creep Wes would be sorry he ever—"

"I don't care about Wes."

"Sure you don't."

Abe knew she could tell everyone on the planet that she didn't care a bit about Wes Vaughn and every single person would believe her . . . except for Megan. She knew better.

"Okay, so I'm a little nervous about the fact that my ex-boyfriend is one of the groomsmen. And I'm a little nervous about seeing him umpteen times over the next four weeks, but it isn't anything I can't handle. I'm over Wes, Megan. Or at least I'm almost over him."

"I know you are, Abe," Megan said. "Almost. But it might be easier if you had a date with a nice guy."

"No it wouldn't. It would just make it all too . . . complicated. Wes would think I was doing it to make him jealous. Then he'd try to make me jealous."

"Most likely."

"I don't like playing games."

Megan smiled in understanding. "I know," she said and patted Abe's hand.

"So," Abe said. "Have we got a deal? I won't tease you about your new name if you don't set me up with anyone at the wedding."

"But . . ."

"Tick tock," Abe said. "Your time is almost up."

"Okay, it's a deal," Megan agreed. "But this doesn't change a thing."

"What do you mean?"

"You'll meet Jack anyway. You're going to fall for him. I just know you will. And I'm still plotting revenge for the four hundred times you've already called me Megan Meegan."

"Yeah?"

"Yeah."

Abe looked at Megan in mock horror. "I'm so scared."

"You should be. You're toast."

Abe tossed back her long strawberry blond hair and shrugged. "Whatever," she said, and then the two women started laughing. The rest of their lunch went by without further teasing or threats.

Chapter Three

"**B**ye, Butt Head," Megan said, giving Abe a quick hug good-bye before she dashed off to the florist for yet another consultation. "I'll see you Saturday night at Mario's."

"I can't wait," Abe said.

"It's just pizza. We've had pizza at Mario's a thousand times."

"I know," Abe said, beaming. "But it'll be so much fun to see everyone together again. I'm really looking forward to it."

Megan just smiled. She knew Abe was nervous about seeing Wes again.

"Hey," Abe said, quickly changing the subject. "Do you have time to go shopping after you meet with the florist? What time is your appointment?"

"I wish I could," Megan said. "I'm meeting Phillip at two-thirty. We're going to go over his checklist one last time. My mother's meeting me there. It might take a while."

"Maybe you'll have some free time afterwards. I'm going to pop over to the mall for a little bit. Call me on my cell if you can meet me later."

"I'll try," Megan said. The longing expression on her face told Abe she would have preferred to skip the florist altogether and go shopping but, alas, she had a wedding to plan. Instead, Megan gave Abe a quick hug and then went off in the opposite direction.

Abe watched her go and felt fortunate that Megan's mother asked to be present at the consultation with the florist. Abe now had the rest of the afternoon to do as she pleased—an unusual event lately. And it was a beautiful day. The sun was warm and shining, and the fresh air felt wonderful.

Abe picked Cameron Village because it was an outdoors shopping center, and she wanted to feel the warm sun shining down on her as she shopped. She spent the next two hours wandering in and out of stores. She didn't buy much, but the free time afforded her the opportunity to think about the upcoming month. It was going to be a busy one, that much was certain, although the previous months had been eventful as well. And the ones before that. Come to think of it, everything about Megan's wedding was busy right from the start. Abe thought back to one occasion in particular. It was a memory that often returned to her, and she didn't know why. Her mind would always wander back to it somehow.

"What color is aubergine?" Abe asked that day last

February when Megan and her bridesmaids went looking at dresses.

"Plum," Megan said, looking through a circular rack of colorful gowns. "What do you think of it?"

"I used purple in my wedding, Megan," Erin, Megan's older sister said matter-of-factly. "No copying."

"I loved your wedding, Erin," Abe said. "Especially the gowns. Everything about them was beautiful."

"I don't know," Susie Keating said. "Didn't Sarah Marshall's bridesmaids wear purple dresses at her wedding? You don't want to use the same color theme as Sarah, Megan. She's got such bad taste."

Erin's big brown eyes narrowed. "What's wrong with purple?"

"Nothing," Susie said quickly. "As long as it's a nice shade of purple. Sarah's dresses had a lot of gray in her purple. It wasn't a pretty color at all. I'm sure the purple you used in your wedding was beautiful, Erin."

Abe bit her tongue to keep from pointing out that the color of Susie's corduroy skirt was gray as well as being way too short for the winter, even if they are in the South.

"Sarah's wedding was pretty," Megan said. "I loved the color of the purple she picked."

"Yeah, but she had the reception in that tacky fire hall. Remember all those purple and pink streamers everywhere? Yuck!"

"They weren't so bad," Taylor said. "What about orange, Megan? That's a good color for a bridesmaid's dress. Everyone loves orange."

"You always want everything to be orange," Chandler accused. "Isn't it enough that you wear orange every other day of the week?"

"I like orange. It's my favorite color."

"We know!" Chandler said. "But that doesn't mean that we have to wear orange gowns for Megan's wedding. Oh, and for the record, Susie, I had a lot of fun at Sarah's wedding."

"The food wasn't that good," Susie said.

"The food was great," Kasey said. "I was Sarah's maid of honor. I know how much work she put into making her wedding day come together. It was wonderful. I think she did a great job."

"Not everyone has the funds for an expensive affair," Megan said curtly. "Sarah was on a tight budget, Susie. Even so, it was a beautiful wedding."

"I guess," Susie shrugged, somewhat miffed that her remarks hadn't won over the other bridesmaids. "All I'm saying is that I wouldn't necessarily have made the same choices."

"It's going to be impossible not to duplicate something someone else has chosen," Chandler said, changing the subject. "I've been a bridesmaid twice in the past six months alone. We've all been to a lot of weddings."

"You can say that again," Abe said. "How many times have you been a bridesmaid since graduation, Meg?"

"I've been in five weddings, not including Erin's," Megan said with authority. "But I was only a bridesmaid in four of them. I did a reading in Ashley's wedding. How about you?"

"Four or five," Abe said. "Including my cousin, remember?"

"Three for me," Kasey said.

"Three for me too," Taylor said. "How about you, Susie?"

"At least that many," Susie said. "But I could be wrong. It's hard to keep count of them all. It's our age, I guess. It seems as if everyone I know is falling in love and taking the plunge."

"Don't knock it 'til you've tried it," Erin said. "Derek and I've been married for three years now and it's not so bad. In fact, I can't imagine anything better. Personally I'm thrilled for my little sister." Megan beamed at her.

"I'd like to try it," Susie said, wistfully. "At least the falling in love part of it. But not everyone finds Mr. Right sitting in the bleacher in front of them at a football game." The last part of her sentence was said in an accusing tone to Megan.

"What do you think of this lilac gown?" Megan said, refusing to take the bait. "It's more suitable for a summer wedding, don't you think?" Susie only looked at her blankly.

It was a sore spot between them. Susie maintained that since she'd spotted Billy first, she should have been afforded the right to first refusal—a theory Megan refused to entertain.

Susie Keating was Megan's friend from work who'd come into the picture when Megan graduated from college two years ago and began working at the magazine. Susie was a graphic artist like Megan, and also like Megan she was very pretty but as far as Abe was concerned that was where their similarities ended. Susie was adorable. Although she too was twenty-four, she could have easily passed for a high school teenager. There was a bouncy, all-American cuteness to her that Abe envied. Her hair was light brown, long, and wavy; she had a way of tossing it when she talked that made it fall around her face to frame it in the best possible light. Her skin was fair and flawless, and there was a natural blush to her cheeks. Her eyes were big and round and a pretty shade of green with flecks of yellow and gray. Susie's eyes twinkled in a way that lit up her face whenever she smiled, which was often. She was shorter than Abe but taller than Megan, and her figure was trim and perfectly proportioned. She had long, athletic legs and a tiny waist she liked to show off by wearing midriff tops. Susie had an outgoing personality and made friends quickly. Initially, Abe liked her almost as much as Megan did, but as time went by she noticed that there was another side to Susie. A side that wasn't always as sweet and smiling as she first appeared.

Several times, Abe saw Susie speak sharply to servers in restaurants, and she once heard her snarl at a cashier in a dress shop—a detail that Abe found troubling. Worse still, Abe noticed that although Susie was always pleasant enough to her, she would often make hurtful remarks about other people when they weren't around. She couldn't help but wonder what Susie said about her when she wasn't there.

"Maybe there will be some single men at the wedding," Taylor offered.

"You already have a boyfriend," Chandler reminded her.

"I know, but I can still flirt, can't I?"

"No."

"Why not?" Susie said. "I hope there will be some cute guys at your wedding, Megan, because I'm planning on doing some flirting myself. I've been going through a dry spell in the dating department. As a matter of fact, I'm glad Taylor brought up the subject. I wanted to let you all know before any of you get any funny ideas—I've got dibs."

"Dibs?" Taylor said. "Dibs on what?"

"Dibs on any cute groomsmen."

"You can't do that," Taylor said. "You can't call dibs on all of them. Why don't you just pick one?" Taylor was a pretty blond with lively blue eyes and a deep, strong voice and yes, it was true, she frequently wore the color orange. Her head was cocked to one side, and she was watching Susie with an expression of bewilderment. "I've never heard of anyone calling dibs on *all* the guys."

"Why not?" Susie said. "You're dating George, Chandler's dating Sean, and Kasey's dating Andrew. Everyone else in the wedding party already has a boyfriend. Come on, guys. Let me have dibs, just this once!"

"That's not fair!" Taylor said, impatiently pushing a strand of hair away from her face. "You can't call dibs on all the groomsmen. That's just being greedy."

"Yeah," Chandler said. "What if Abe likes one of them? You forgot about her. Is she supposed to step back just because you called dibs on everyone? All's fair in love and war, you know."

"But Abe already dated Wes," Susie whined. "Why can't I have a shot at him?"

"If you're attracted to Wes, why don't you just say so?" Erin asked, mildly amused by the youthful drama unfolding before her.

"Yeah," Chandler said. "We didn't know you liked Wes. Why didn't you tell us?"

"I don't know if I do or not," Susie said, exasperated. "I don't know him well enough to make that decision yet . . . but I'd like to get to know him better. Maybe I'll like him, maybe I won't."

Abe felt her cheeks redden at the sound of his dreaded name. "Be my guest, Susie."

"See!" Susie said triumphantly. "Abe doesn't care if I call dibs on Wes."

"Of course she doesn't care if you call dibs on Wes," Chandler said. "She probably thinks you have a screw loose for calling dibs on Wes! But he isn't the only eligible groomsman. What about the other guy?"

"What other guy?"

"Billy's friend. What's his name?"

"Jack," Megan said. "You'd like Jack, Abe."

"Dibs!" Susie shouted.

"Abe has dibs on Jack!" Megan shouted back.

"Sorry, Abe," Susie said. "But I called him first."

"Greedy, greedy, greedy," Taylor said. "Next thing, you'll call dibs on all the male guests!"

"I'm just keeping my options open," Susie said. "You don't mind if I call dibs on Jack too, do you, Abe?"

"No. Not at all. Knock yourself out."

"Okay, I will," Susie said, and everyone laughed.

"Susie," Erin scolded. "You really are a brat."

"I know," she grinned. "But like Chandler said, all's fair in love and war."

Abe stopped by the coffee bar for a caramel frappuccino and enjoyed its creamy deliciousness while she replayed the events of that winter shopping trip. Dibs? She wondered what Susie meant by that. Did she want first crack at every male in the wedding? The notion seemed outrageous to Abe, considering that she was calling dibs on living, breathing human beings—not the last chocolate in the box or the front seat of the car. Besides, other than Jack, Susie knew all the groomsmen in the wedding. Abe mentally ran down the list: there was Alex, Megan's cousin. Nice guy, but he was three years younger and too much like a brother to think of him as a romantic prospect. Then there was George, Taylor's boyfriend. Then Nathan, Billy's brother, but he's only fifteen and, as such, unavailable. Then there was Derek, Erin's husband but he's six years older and, of course, married. There were only two groomsmen remaining and since Susie hadn't met Jack either, the only person her request for "dibs" could be meant for was Wes Vaughn. Wes.

Wesley was his given name, but no one called him that. Everyone knew him as Wes, and the thought of him made Abe's knees feel shaky. She could remember everything about him in perfect detail, even though it had been weeks since the last time she'd seen him. He was tall and blond and had that all-American look that made women immediately go insane. His eyes were brown and smiling, and when he looked at Abe she felt like melting. Dangerously attractive was the way Abe's mother described him. Hot was the way Abe saw him.

They'd dated briefly the year before. It was a romance that started out well but ended in disaster and, even now, Abe still didn't know what went wrong. The entire relationship lasted five months, but in emotional-investment time, it felt to Abe like years. He'd swept her off her feet in a way that still made her feel woozy.

"Be careful," Billy told her. "Wes is one of my best friends, and he's . . . I mean, he's a great guy and all. Don't get me wrong. It's just that he's . . . well, he's kind of a ladies' man, if you know what I mean. Wes isn't ready to settle down yet."

Of course, one look in Wes's big brown eyes was all Abe needed to forget all about Billy's warning. She fell head over heels for him. She didn't throw herself at him—that wasn't her style. For the first few months, Abe was happy to get to know Wes. And the more she got to know of him, the more she liked him. He was romantic and attentive and he called with the required frequency, not too much and not too little. He brought her flowers and told her she was beautiful. He even had a bright red, flashy sports car that made her feel like a million bucks when she rode in it. Wes made Abe feel happy, and she loved just being with him.

But then things changed. One day Wes suddenly stopped calling. Abe grew concerned after a few days passed without a single word. Was he sick? Had something bad happened to him? She called him but instead of finding a boyfriend who needed her help, he greeted her with cool indifference. "I've been busy," he said.

"Oh," Abe said surprised. "What's going on? Is it something I can help you with?"

"No," he said.

Abe waited for him to say more, but he didn't. "Okay," she said. "Well, I guess I'll see you at Billy's place this weekend."

"I don't know if I'll be there. I may not make it."

"Wes, you're acting weird," she said, more confused than ever. "What's up with that?"

He sighed. "All right, Abe. If you must know, I think we should start to see other people."

The statement caught her offguard and she didn't know how to respond. "Oh?" she finally said. "Why?"

"I don't have a reason," he said, and once again there was that coolness to his voice and another long pause. "Look," he said, hesitantly. "You and I've had fun together over the past few months, but I think it's time we went our separate ways." It was Abe's turn to be silent and she waited for him to explain himself, but he obviously was in no hurry to do so. After another tortuously long pause he said, "It's just that I . . . I can't help the way I feel. I like you, Abe. You're a great girl, but I feel like we need a break from each other. I'll call you after I get my head clear." There was another long, stony silence until Abe realized he wasn't going to say anything else.

"Okay," she said as calmly as she could. "Bye." Then she hung up the phone. Wes never called again, and neither did she.

Even now, months later, the painful memory of that phone conversation was still fresh. The three or four times she'd seen him since then were awkward and bewildering. Wes would smile at her with a mournful look in his eyes and say: "How ya doing, Abe? It's good to see you. I've missed you a lot." Or, worse yet, he'd reminisce about their short, but still so sweet, romance. "Remember when we went hiking, Abe? That was fun, wasn't it?" Sometimes, he'd suggest that they should get together again, always with that same sad, yearning expression on his face. Abe would hesitate at first, but then allow herself to open up to him again. He was so charming and so handsome. Eventually, she'd find herself relaxing her guard with Wes, and then she'd smile at him. Once or twice, she'd even flirted with him! "I'll call you," he promised. But, of course, he never did.

Abe heard through the grapevine about the three girl-friends Wes dated since her. "He's an idiot," Megan exclaimed. "I'm sorry you ever met him. He's such a creep! I'd have him kicked out of the wedding, but Billy won't let me. Wes is one of his best friends but I'll never understand why. Billy says Wes has a good side; he's just a lousy boyfriend. And he's immature! I'm sorry, Abe. Would you like me to arrange to have one or both of his legs broken? He can't very well be a groomsman on crutches, now can he? I don't want you to feel awkward at the wedding."

"It's okay," Abe told her, not doubting for a minute that she'd do it. "Wes isn't the last guy in the world. I'll live."

"I know it," her best friend said. "And you're not the type of person who curls up and dies just because of some jerk."

"Darn right!" Abe said, pushing away the thought of Wes's smile. "Besides, Wes and I aren't enemies. We'll be fine at the wedding. Don't worry about us. We're both adults, right?"

"Well, you are. I'm not so sure about Wes."

"It doesn't matter. He's ancient history. It didn't work out. It happens. Big deal."

Abe sighed, her thoughts slowly returning to the afternoon of shopping that lay before her. She picked up a blue candle from the display shelf in the candle shop and sniffed it. It was dreadful. She picked up a red one and did the same thing, wrinkling her nose at the pungent aroma. Her thoughts weren't on shopping for candles. "Susie can have him," she said aloud, causing another customer to look at her with an alarmed expression.

"Sorry," Abe said. "Don't mind me. I'm just thinking out loud. To tell you the truth, I'm not sure if Susie even wants him. She might want the guy who just moved back from Seattle."

"Oh," the customer said and backed away from her slowly.

"Personally, I think she wants to keep all her options open. Just in case one doesn't pan out."

"Probably," the customer said and bolted for the door. Abe shrugged. Maybe Susie had her eye on the other guy and not Wes after all. What was his name? Jack. That's it.

Billy had known the mysterious Jack since childhood, in much the same way that Megan had known Abe. After graduation Jack attended the University of Washington. Abe heard Billy mention his name a few times. It was always "Jack and I came here to kayak once" or "Jack says the beaches here are just as good as the beaches on the West Coast." Megan met him once when he blew into town for a whirlwind three-day visit and talked about him for days afterwards. Abe vaguely remembered a photo of him hanging on the wall in Billy's apartment, or at least she assumed it was him. It was a picture of a group of people at a party. Everyone was wearing red sweaters and there was a Christmas tree in the background. Abe recognized most of the people except for a blurry, smiling dark-haired man who stood behind Billy. Maybe that was Jack but, if so, it was hard to tell what he looked like from the photo. No matter; Abe didn't feel particularly curious about him. Or anyone else for that matter. Ever since Wes unceremoniously dumped her, the only romance she'd allowed in her life was those awful blind dates Billy and Megan orchestrated. No wonder a long, peaceful break from dating was so appealing.

Abe picked up a yellow candle that was labeled *Sunflower Field* and sniffed it. Mmm. Yummy. That was more like it. She made her way to the cash register. A long, bubble bath with the sweet-smelling candle burning nearby sounded like the perfect way to end a long day.

Chapter Four

FRIDAY, JUNE 1

Abe examined herself in the mirror with a critical eye and sighed at her reflection. She practiced smiling and tilting her chin in appealing ways for a while before she stuck out her tongue and crossed her eyes. "Blaa," she said to the mirror. It was going to be a thorny evening and no amount of smiling and head tilting could change that.

"It'll be fun," Megan said when she'd called a half-hour earlier. "I promise."

Abe giggled with her, as if spending the evening with her ex-boyfriend was the most fun she could possibly hope for. "It'll be awesome!" she gushed. "You're going to look so cute in your new shirt."

"And Billy-boy on my arm."

"That too."

Secretly, Abe was nervous. The next four weeks were going to be chock full of pre-wedding, wedding, and post-wedding events, all of which would include Wes Vaughn. And Susie Keating. And Jack, whoever he was. Tonight's dinner at the pizza parlor was the kickoff to it all. Next was a barbecue at the Randals' house, then the bridal shower (coed, naturally), then the rehearsal along with the requisite dinner, then, finally, the wedding. Abe sighed. It's going to be a long, long month.

Abe continued to mug for the mirror, lost in her thoughts. Part of her dreaded the next few weeks, especially those awkward first moments of seeing Wes again—smiling as if she didn't care one little bit that he was gorgeous and that he used to be her boyfriend. Yet, another part of her felt excited. It was such an exciting time in Megan's life. How could Abe not see it as the thrilling venture that it was? There was also this funny butterfly feeling in Abe's stomach. It had been there, mostly at quieter moments, for the past few weeks. She didn't know where it came from or what it meant, but it was there and it was persistent. It was a hopeful feeling of anticipation, almost like she knew something wonderful was about to happen to her. Abe dismissed it as a case of maid-of-honor jitters although deep in her heart she hoped there was more to it than that.

She carefully pulled her long strawberry blond hair up into a loose bun, pulling a few curled tresses from behind her ear in hopes it would give her that carefree-but-sophisticated look. This was a procedure that rarely went well because her hair was more wispy than sophisticated. After several tries, she finally gave up and let her hair fall loose down her back.

"That's going to have to do," she sighed. She was wearing a long, black, knit skirt and a bright pink floral top with wide bell sleeves. It was a new outfit and even if she said so herself, it looked nice on her. Her long hair was soft and shining, and she wore just the right amount of makeup to give her a fresh-scrubbed, clean look. She wanted to be sure Wes knew she wasn't trying to impress him, but she also wanted him to know that she was doing just fine (thank you very much) without him. Longing for a lost love was too tenth grade for Abe Gibson to consider. She checked herself in the mirror one last time before she headed down the stairs.

The phone rang just as she walked into the kitchen. Abe winked at her mother who was finishing up with the dinner dishes. It was Megan on the line . . . again.

"Are you ready yet?"

"Yep. I was just getting ready to walk out the door."

"Good. This will be the last chance for us all to be able to have fun and relax before the wedding happenings begin—so don't be late!"

"I know and let me say, it's working. You seem very relaxed. Not stressed out one little bit."

"Ha, ha," Megan said. "For your information, smarty pants, I am relaxed. I'm so relaxed I'll probably take a nap there."

"I can tell," Abe said.

"And don't forget you're going to meet Jack."

"I remember."

"Don't be late. I don't want Susie snarking on him before you get there."

"I'm really hungry," Abe said, changing the subject. "Aren't you?"

"And don't wolf down your food when we get there! Be ladylike, for a change."

"Ha!"

"What are you wearing anyway?"

"You'll see," Abe said.

"Oh, Abe," Megan said. "I can't wait for you to meet him. You're going to just go insane. He's so hot."

"Don't start with me, Megan!" Abe shouted into the phone causing her mother to raise her eyebrows.

"All right, all right. I'll stop. Just don't be late."

"I won't."

"See you in twenty."

"See you then."

Abe hung up the phone, rolling her eyes at her mother.

"What's Megan up to now?" Mrs. Gibson asked.

"No good, as usual."

"That girl," Mrs. Gibson said, shaking her head. "Poor Billy. I hope he knows he's marrying a tiger."

"Poor Billy! How about poor me?"

"You'll do fine." Of course, Abe hadn't told her mother about her worries over Wes. She didn't have to. Her mother always knew when she was troubled by something, no matter how big or small. Mrs. Gibson reached over and gave her daughter a hug.

"Don't worry about that bozo, honey. You're going to show him a thing or two about what class is."

"I'm not worried. Tonight will be fun."

"It's all for Megan, and she's worth it. You're a good friend, Abe."

"I am, aren't I?"

"I like your new outfit."

"Thanks."

"You look so pretty," said Mrs. Gibson, continuing with the string of compliments.

"Thanks, Mom, but I think you may be a bit biased. Oh, and by the way, starting tonight I'm not Abe anymore. I'm Abigail."

"Abigail? You hate that name."

"I know, but Mrs. Randal thinks Abe is too informal for Megan's wedding. She thinks Abigail is far more sophisticated. She requested that I make the necessary changes."

"Change your name?" Mrs. Gibson said. "Is that so? Would you like me to call her and remind her that everyone knows you as Abe?"

"Nah," Abe said. "That's okay. It's just until after the wedding. Besides, if Megan can't get her to budge, what makes you think you can?"

"Good point. We both know where Megan gets her stubborn streak, don't we? Very well then, Abigail, have a good time. Will you be late tonight?"

Abe's mother forgot about any curfew rules four months ago when Abe moved back home. She'd lived at a nearby apartment for two years but it proved to be expensive and noisy. She was already considering moving back home when a series of highly publicized break-ins occurred in her apartment complex. Abe's older brother, Rex, recently landed his dream job as a computer programmer for a medical research company in San Diego and Abe's worried parents offered her his large, spacious bedroom. After a lot of thought, she accepted their offer. She hadn't regretted the decision, despite the occasional concerns that she should be more independent. She was determined to make the move back home work for her in a big way. She paid her parents rent and was still able to put most of her paychecks into a savings account. She hoped that she'd someday have enough for a down payment on a condo or a townhouse of her own. Maybe even an old fixer-upper in Raleigh if she could find one that was affordable. The endeavor was putting a crimp on Abe's clothes shopping, but watching the balance of her savings account grow was worth as much as the good feeling of wearing a funky new pair of shoes. Almost.

Abe liked living with her parents, although she was hesitant to admit it. So many of her friends were getting married and moving into homes of their own. She worried that she should be one of them. But her childhood home was comfortable and familiar, and her parents were better company than any roommate she'd ever had. There were never any disagreements over rules because Abe rarely abused them. She paid her rent on time, mowed the lawn, made dinner twice a week, did the dishes most nights, and helped with the house cleaning. She was so helpful, her father took to calling her Cinderella.

"I'll be home by ten," Abe told her mother.

"Why so early?"

"It's just pizza at Mario's. We're going to meet Billy's long lost friend finally."

"Who's that?"

"Jack?"

"Jack? Jack who?"

"I don't know his last name. He's an old friend of Billy's. He moved away about five years ago. Now he's come back here to live." Mrs. Gibson smiled at her daughter. Abe had a way of speaking in a flamboyant, dramatic way—especially when she was speaking with a loved one. Her eyes would sparkle and her voice would boom, as if what was happening right at that moment was the most exciting thing that ever happened to her. Mrs. Gibson also knew that the more nervous Abe was, the more animated she became.

"Calm down, sweetie," Mrs. Gibson said, smiling at her daughter's dramatics. "It'll be good to see everyone tonight. Try to have fun."

"Oh, yeah, it'll be a laugh a minute," Abe said, shooing her hand. "Especially with Susie Keating flirting with every man in the room. It'll be awesome." She rolled her eyes one last time, then headed down the hallway.

"Well I hope you do some flirting of your own!" her mother called after her. "Put a little wiggle in that walk, girl!"

"Mom!"

The restaurant was crowded by the time Abe arrived. The chairs lining the long table Megan reserved were almost full. Chandler was already there with her boyfriend, Sean, and Taylor was with her boyfriend, George. Megan and Billy hadn't arrived yet. Nor had Susie Keating or . . . Wes.

Abe didn't know whether or not to be happy that Wes wasn't there. It saved her the embarrassment of him seeing her walk into the restaurant alone, but now she had the pleasure of sitting there like a dope and feigning nonchalance when he walked into the room. Maybe he wouldn't show up.

"Hi," Abe said, cheerfully tossing back her long hair and sitting in the chair next to Chandler.

"Howdy," Chandler said. "Are you ready for the fun to begin?"

"Yes!" Abe said with gusto. "I can't wait to see Megan walk down the aisle!"

Sean wrinkled his nose as if he smelled something bad. "Better Billy than me," he said, smiling at Chandler.

"Gross," she said, tossing back her long hair. "As if anyone in their right mind would marry you." Sean just shrugged. It was a demonstration that fooled no one. It was of popular opinion that Chandler and Sean would be the next ones in line for wedded bliss but, so far anyway, neither one would say.

Just then a group of people arrived. Kasey and her boyfriend, Andrew, walked in with Alex, Nathan, Susie and . . . Wes. There was a buzz of conversation and happy laughter that surrounded them. Abe planted a big smile on her face. "Hey there," she laughed, waving happily to the newcomers and keeping her eyes focused on Kasey.

"Hey," Kasey said. She knew all about Abe's sad saga with Wes, and she still wasn't prepared to forgive him. She tolerated him only for Megan's and Billy's sake but, otherwise, she might have given him a piece of her mind—a fate Abe didn't wish on anyone, even Wes. Kasey took the seat next to her after she gave her a big, warm bear hug. Andrew sat down next to Kasey. Now Abe had Chandler on one side of her and Kasey on the other. She was surrounded by friends.

"Hi beautiful," a voice that was all-too familiar said from behind her.

"Hi," Abe said enthusiastically, barely looking over her shoulder. But she had to look at him, if only to prove to him and everyone else at the table that she was completely over him. Hundred percent over him. She couldn't be any more over him if she tried. She was totally over him.

Abe held her breath and smiled as brightly as she could, but not too brightly. She didn't want to gush. That wouldn't do either. But, darn it, he was still as achingly good-looking as ever. Wes stood behind her chair, saying hello to everyone and, as he talked, he let his hand fall lightly on Abe's shoulder. "You look great," he whispered in her ear when the greetings were done.

"Thanks," she said—again with a bit too much cheer. She bit the inside of her mouth. She was trying too hard.

"Sit over here, Wes," Susie said from across the table. "Megan and Billy will be here any second. They're bringing the man of mystery."

"Man of mystery?" he said. "Who's that?"

"Jack, remember?"

"Oh, yeah. I heard he was back in town." Abe noticed an expression on Wes's handsome face that she couldn't identify, and noted the sudden coolness of his voice. Kasey looked at Abe and smiled a devilish smile. Her eyes said it all—perhaps there was some history between Wes and Jack that would prove to be interesting. Wes took the empty chair next to Susie and immediately turned his full attention to her. Abe was relieved he was no longer behind her, but the memory of his fingertips touching her back lingered on long after he was gone.

Susie looked absolutely gorgeous in a beautiful turquoise print blouse and a short turquoise tiered skirt that showed off her nice legs. Abe noted that Susie's hair was done up in a sophisticated, but exquisitely messy bun—the same sort of bun she'd failed to accomplish earlier. She also noticed that Wes and Susie somehow looked good together.

His all-American handsomeness complimented Susie's cheerleader cuteness perfectly. They looked like they could be on the cover of a magazine modeling clothes for cool, sophisticated, perfect people.

"What's new?" Kasey asked, pulling Abe's attention back to where it belonged.

"Not much," she said, smiling. She was smiling so much tonight her cheeks were starting to ache. "I'm just trying to keep up with Megan."

"How long is her list of demands now?"

"We're down to just two pages, but things could get ugly any time now."

"It's a good thing she has you for her maid of honor. I'd have been fired by now."

"It's not so bad," Abe said. "I like helping her with

the planning. The shopping is a lot of fun, as long as we don't cross Megan's mom. Then we'd have trouble. I never knew there was so much involved with a wedding. It's crazy."

Kasey smiled, letting her gaze drift over to Susie and Wes. "Are you okay?" she asked gently.

"I'm great," Abe said with all the sincerity she could muster.

"How about Erin? She's Megan's sister. Shouldn't she be the matron of honor?"

"Erin's married, working full time, and taking classes at night school. She also lives an hour away. She's an honorary matron of honor who's been given a reprieve. Erin's helping plenty though. She's helping me plan the wedding shower and the bachelorette party. And don't ask about what her mother is making her do."

"Whew!" Kasey said. "This wedding stuff isn't for wimps, is it? Erin's a good sister, and you're a good friend, Abe."

"Thanks." Abe said and smiled a real smile. Leave it to Kasey to make her feel good.

That's when the rest of the group arrived. Billy and Megan walked in then with a few stragglers. Megan Randal never entered a room without everyone noticing. All her entrances were grand because she possessed a flair for drama that few could equal.

"Hi!" she shouted, bouncing up to the table. "Is everyone here?"

"Almost," Billy said, looking around the table. "I don't see Jack."

"Here I am," a voice said from behind Abe. She

looked around and saw him and felt, if only for a second, a pang of disappointment—he wasn't as handsome as Wes.

"Hey, buddy," Billy said. "Do you know everyone?"

"No," Jack said, looking around the table. "Not everyone. I know Nathan, of course, and Caroline." Jack nodded at each of the mentioned persons. "And I know Matthew."

People greeted Jack warmly. The men stood and shook his hand, and the women smiled up at him and said hello.

"This is Chandler," Billy said. "And her boyfriend, Sean. Chandler's a good friend of Megan's and a bridesmaid."

"Hello," Chandler said.

"Nice to meet you," Sean added.

"This is Taylor and George. They're both in the wedding."

"Hey," Jack said, shaking everyone's hand. "It's nice to meet you."

"This is Alex, Megan's cousin."

"Hey, Alex."

"Hi. Nice to meet you."

"And, of course, you know Wes."

"Yeah," Jack said, but Abe detected a slight hesitation to the greeting. "How's it going, Wes?"

"Great," Wes said, with an expression that could only be described as a smirk.

Kasey gave Abe another meaningful look. "This is getting interesting," she whispered in Abe's ear.

"This is Susan Keating," Billy continued. Megan was

standing next to him with her hand clutching his elbow. "She works with Megan. She's a graphic artist too."

"Nice to meet you, Susan," Jack said, shaking her hand.

"Nice to meet you too, Jack," Susie said, standing to shake his hand. "I hear you lived here in Raleigh a few years ago."

"Yes," Jack said. "I'm from Chapel Hill. After high school, I went to the University of Washington. There was a job opening at IBM in Seattle after I graduated and I took it. It's taken me a while to find the right job so I could transfer to North Carolina, but now I'm back to stay."

"You didn't like it in Seattle?"

"I loved it," he said. "But I missed it here. It's good to be back on the East Coast."

Susie gave her one of her irresistible smiles." I'm glad you're back," she said and Abe noticed a look of disgusted annoyance on Wes's face.

"This is Kasey and her boyfriend, Andrew." Billy told Jack, pointing him toward the other side of the long table.

"Kasey . . . Andrew," Jack said, shaking hands.

"Nice to meet you," all three said at the same time, then laughed.

"And this is Abe . . . a . . . gail. Abigail," Billy said. Abe could see that Megan's hand was still clamped to his elbow in a death grip. "She's Megan's maid of honor."

Abe looked into his face and smiled. "Hi," she said. There was something about his face that seemed to draw her in. He had a warm, friendly openness to his expression that made her feel suddenly odd, almost speechless.

His hair was brown and he wore it long and moppy, just the way she liked it. He had warm brown eyes and long, dark eyelashes and a welcoming, friendly smile. He also had the biggest dimples Abe had ever seen.

"Hi, Abe-a-gail," Jack said. "It's nice to meet you."

"It's Abigail," she said, letting the dreaded name fall from her tongue. She extended her hand and he took it, peering at her with interest. "Nice to meet you," she said, trying to keep her voice steady. What was wrong with her? A minute ago she was disappointed that he wasn't as handsome as Wes. Now she was as tongue-tied as a teenager.

Jack held her hand for a long moment, shaking it cordially. Abe liked the way her hand felt in his, and she liked his brown eyes. She felt a sudden lump in her throat. "Hi, Abigail," he said again. His voice was low and wonderful.

"Everyone," Billy said, breaking through Abe's fog. "Meet Jack. Jack, meet everyone."

He gave a final wave and then looked around the table for an empty chair. Abe keenly felt his absence and right away began wishing he'd come back. Of course, the only chairs left were across on the other side of the table, near Megan and Billy and . . . Wes . . . and . . . Susie.

"Abigail," Megan called to her from across the noisy room. "Come over here and talk to me!"

"No," Abe called back playfully. "You come over here and talk to me!"

"No, you come here!"

"No, you!"

This went back and forth for several minutes good-naturedly. Finally, Abe stood up and went to Megan's side of the table. The pizza hadn't arrived yet, she reasoned, and the heck with Wes. She could talk to Megan if she wanted to, right?

"Quit your bellowing," Abe said, sliding into the seat next to Megan. "What's so important anyway?"

"Nothing," Megan smiled coyly. "I just wanted you to come over."

"I'll only stay until the pizza gets here," she said. "I'm starving, remember."

Later, Abe couldn't remember a single word of her conversation with Megan. All she would recall was the way her heart pounded whenever she glanced over toward Jack. And the feeling of being off-balance and having knees made of rubber. She remembered talking to Megan, all the while smiling, but her mind was on someone else. And it wasn't Wes. Suddenly, all her worries over seeing him again were gone like mist in the sunshine.

"Hi, *Abigail*," Susie, said.

"Hi, *Susan*," Abe said. Susie was in bliss because Wes was on one side of her and Jack was on the other. Abe had never seen her look happier.

Wes squinted his eyes at Abe for a second. "What's going on here?" he asked.

"Nothing," Megan said, giving him a look that could melt metal. "We're just getting prepared for the wedding. That's all."

"Huh?" Wes said. "What's with the names?" Then an expression of understanding crossed his face. "Oh," he said. "Okay. I get it."

"You get what?" Susie asked, but Megan launched into a discussion about the many upcoming activities that everyone would be attending, and Abe never did learn exactly what *it* was that Wes got.

Abe stifled her sigh of relief when the waiter finally brought the pizzas. She suspected that Megan's real reason for calling her over was so that she could show off in front of Wes. Of course, she didn't know that Abe was irreversibly over Wes from the second she looked into Jack's eyes. When Abe arrived back at her chair, she sat down, a smile still frozen on her face. It wasn't easy pretending to be giddily happy for an extended period of time—especially since she felt as if she'd been struck by some kind of crazy lightening.

She supposed that she'd done a good job with her performance, however, because Megan gave her a triumphant smile from across the room. Her expression made Abe hopeful that her case of nerves had gone unnoticed by her friends—at least Megan seemed to think so. Abe could almost hear her do one of their old high school cheers. Mission accomplished. Abe—1, Wes—zip.

Abe ate her pizza although she wasn't nearly as hungry as she claimed to be. She talked to Kasey and Andrew as they ate and tried to recover from the sudden, new feelings that were crashing down on top of her. She was careful not to look across the table. She was soon able to convince herself that all of the excitement of the evening had caught up to her. Yep, that must be it. She was having some kind of maid-of-honor breakdown. It was probably quite common. She made a mental note to research the matter on the Internet when she got home. She'd be fine in a few minutes.

"So," a voice said from her left. "Megan tells me you work at the bank." She hadn't seen him sit down next to her in the chair formerly occupied by Chandler, who'd finished eating and was now on the other side of the table talking with Alex and Nathan.

"Oh, hi," Abe said, swallowing a bite of pizza. "Yes, I'm in the Auditing Department."

"Really?" Jack said. "I'm an accountant myself. I work for IBM. I start Monday at their office in Raleigh."

"Our bank has done some work with them," Abe said, her mouth suddenly dry. *What a dumb thing to say,* she told herself. "We have quite a few clients who work there as well," she added and smiled. He smiled back and Abe tried to ignore the instant pounding of her heart and the sudden flutter in her stomach. Maid-of-honor psychosis was probably what it was called, she thought, wanting to jot down the phrase for future reference.

"Billy and Megan have told me a lot of good things about you."

"Thanks. They speak well of you too." She was starting to think that if she didn't stop smiling like an idiot soon, her face was going to permanently freeze that way.

"I bet they do," Jack said. "Probably a little too much."

"What do you mean?" she asked. This couldn't all be her imagination, could it? Was there really this . . . chemistry between them?

"I think they're trying to match us up," Jack said, leaning closer to her. Abe almost swooned but decided it probably wasn't the time or place. Then another thought came to her—a thought that made her heart drop. Maybe she was the only one who felt this way. Maybe to Jack, she was just another face in the crowd.

"They've been known to do that," Abe said, pushing aside the thought. "Don't get me started about Billy and Megan's matchmaking."

"You too, huh? I've been in town for two days, and Billy has my calendar set for the next month. Every weekend is booked already. I think he set up this party tonight just so I could meet everyone."

"That's what I was told to be here for."

Jack shook his head and grinned. "I guess I don't mind. It's great to be back, but it isn't the same circle of friends that it was six years ago. There are a lot of new faces here. I'm happy to meet everyone. It's just that I'd rather not be the center of attention so close to their wedding day. I'd rather the fuss be for them."

He was looking deeply into Abe's eyes with a searching, curious expression on his face. "We'd probably be here anyway," she said, trying to find words that weren't as stupid as they sounded. "I mean at Mario's. We come here a lot. Don't worry about Megan and Billy getting their fair share of attention; Megan always steals the show. And you're not going to have time for anything but making a fuss over them."

"I know. There's a barbecue tomorrow, right?"

"Right."

"Then there's a wedding shower next week. . . . Since when do guys go to wedding showers? What's up with that?"

"You mean the Jack and Jill shower?"

"Is that what it's called?"

"Yes," Abe smiled. "Why should the girls have all the fun? It's at my house."

"Great. I've never been to a wedding shower before. You'll have to tell me how to behave."

"You'll do fine," Abe said. He was so nice and so friendly, she was starting to relax. "We'll drink fruit punch and play bingo using the letters B-I-L-L-Y. Then Megan and Billy will open up about a thousand presents and after that, we'll eat cake and glue all the bows onto a paper plate to make a pretend bouquet Megan can use at the rehearsal. It'll be fun."

On Jack's face was an expression of fascinated horror. "Fun?"

"Don't worry," Abe said. "There will be lots of food and beer."

"Okay," he grinned. "I could survive that, somehow. After that, we have the rehearsal, right?"

"Yep," Abe said. "And the dinner afterwards, of course. Then, the next day is the wedding."

"Yeah, the wedding." They were looking into each other's eyes and the feeling of being somehow off-balance returned to Abe. It was an odd, floating feeling, as if they were drinking up the sight of each other. The thought flashed through her mind that she couldn't possibly be the only one who felt it.

"How do you like being back in Raleigh?" she asked, swallowing the lump in her throat.

"So far, so good," he said. "It's much better than I remember."

"Really?"

"Yes," he said, studying her. He cleared his throat and smiled. "But a lot's changed around here. I don't remember this restaurant being here before. Wasn't this an empty field?"

"Yes," Abe said. "It's only been here for a few years. The whole block is new. Raleigh is a boom town."

"It's like that in Seattle too," Jack said. "Except we have more rain."

"How long were you there?"

"Almost six years, but I can't believe it was that long ago that I moved away."

"Will you miss it?"

"A little. I have some good friends in Seattle, but I like being back on the East Coast. Washington never felt . . . permanent somehow. I always knew I'd be back here someday." He was looking into her eyes again. Abe returned the gaze, and he leaned closer to her. "I'm glad I did," he said, staring into her face. Her heart was pounding and her breathing was uneven.

"Hi," the voice from behind them pulled Abe out of her spell. Susie Keating placed her perfectly manicured hand on Jack's shoulder and said, "I just wanted to be sure you were having a good time, Jack. I know what it's like to be the new kid in town. I moved here from Greensboro a few years ago." Susie giggled and Abe fought a sharp, sudden stab of annoyance.

"Thanks," Jack said. "I appreciate that. I'm having a good time. Thank you."

Susie then launched into a conversation about Raleigh and how much it had changed over the past few years. She was animated and funny and there was a lilt to her voice that was almost like listening to music. And, Abe thought, Jack was listening all too intently. In fact, it seemed as if he'd all but forgotten about everyone else in the room, including her.

"You know," Susie said. "I bet you're having trouble finding your way around."

"I've managed," he said. "But yes, things are different than they were before."

"Oh, no," she said. "I can't let you wander around town like a lost puppy. I'll tell you what; I'm free all day tomorrow. How about I pick you up a couple of hours before the barbecue and give you a tour of the new Raleigh?"

Jack was momentarily caught offguard by her offer. "Oh, um . . ." he said and looked quickly at Abe.

"You should go," Abe said, smiling from ear to ear. "Susie knows Raleigh inside and out."

"Well, I did grow up here. I'm sure I'll figure it out."

"But it's changed so much," Susie said. "Come on, let me show you around. It'll be fun."

"Umm . . ."

"It's settled then," Susie cooed. "I'll pick you up at

noon. The barbecue doesn't start until four o'clock. We'll have plenty of time for a quick tour around town."

"Okay," Jack said.

"See you then," Susie said. She turned to leave but before she did, she gave Abe a quick smile. "See you later, Abigail," she said, looking like the proverbial cat that swallowed the canary.

Chapter Five

Abe awoke at the ungodly hour of 6:00 to a blaring noise that was coming from her alarm clock. Somehow she must have accidentally turned the button to ON the night before. So there she was, wide awake at the crack of dawn on a Saturday morning. A light rain quickly and quietly passed through town the night before, and Abe could tell by the scent of the sweet, fresh air coming from the open window in her bedroom that it was going to be another perfect day.

She didn't want to get out of bed, but the likelihood of falling back to sleep softly slipped away from her. She was now fully awake even though she was still curled up underneath the blankets. Perhaps it was the sudden, rude awakening that morning, but Abe felt there was something amiss about her world. She reminded herself that she could easily go back to sleep by snuggling against her soft, warm pillows, but that didn't help. Not really. She couldn't ignore the nagging feeling of unease that crept into the edges of her mind and refused to go away. Something inside of her was telling her that it was going to be one of those days.

She pushed back the covers and stared at the ceiling. Abe was angry. She'd woken up that way and didn't know why—or at least that's what she told herself—but memories of Susie Keating's parting smile and the hazy, off-center feeling she experienced after meeting Jack still occupied her thoughts. She lay in bed and tried to reason with herself in an effort to somehow shake off the uncharacteristic bad mood that crept over her, but the feeling of unease didn't go away.

It's just all the fuss and excitement going on in her life right now, she told herself for the umpteenth time as she stared at her dark ceiling. Watching her best friend get married was turning out to be an emotional process. Clearly it had all finally caught up with her and manifested itself into swooning over a stranger. She must have romance on the brain. Why else had she gone so far over the deep end in such a short period of time?

Abe sighed and got out of bed. She put on a pair of gym socks and slipped into her well-worn, but perfectly comfortable bathrobe and crept downstairs to make a pot of coffee. She tried to put her mind on other things, but images of Jack (and his dimples) kept popping into her head. It was still too dark to sit out on the screened-in porch and read the newspaper, as was her usual Saturday-morning custom. Even with the lights on, it was dark and chilly. Instead, she contented herself with reading the paper at the kitchen table. Of course she was too distracted to give attention to the articles she read. The woes of the world seemed remote to her today. She accidentally bumped her hand against her coffee mug and sloshed coffee on the sports page—a blooper she was certain wouldn't please her father.

Finally, she decided to make use of the time and make breakfast. Surely cooking would take her thoughts away from Susie's "tour" with Jack. Abe pulled out the big black griddle from the island cabinet and set it on the stove. Yes, that was the answer. A plate of pancakes always made her happy again. Pancakes make everyone happy.

A half hour later, she'd prepared stacks of pancakes and fried a half pound of bacon. She'd even chopped up a cantaloupe and scrambled what was left of the eggs. "Breakfast," Abe called up the steps. "Come and get it while it's hot!" She didn't worry about waking anyone too early. Her parents were always up with the birds.

"What's this?" her father said, marching into the kitchen. "What are you doing up so early? Don't princesses sleep in on Saturdays?"

"Pipe down," Abe scolded him, "or I'll give your share to Bailey." The Gibson's ancient terrier looked up at her with hopeful brown eyes.

"I wouldn't dream of upsetting you, my darling. And Bailey doesn't get pancakes. Eggs and bacon are all she'll require this morning."

"Oh my," Mrs. Gibson purred a few minutes later when she arrived in the kitchen. "Something smells good. Could it be? Oh, it is! Pancakes! I love pancakes. How nice. Thank you, baby."

"I'm glad someone appreciates me," Abe said and allowed her mother to give her a peck on the cheek.

"I appreciate you," her father said. "Especially when you cook for me. I'll tell you what. Just so you know how grateful I am, your mother will do the dishes for you."

"You're quite a guy," Abe said.

"I am, aren't I? What gets you up and about so early this morning?"

"My stupid alarm clock went off, and I couldn't get back to sleep."

"I heard you down here banging around the kitchen. I was wondering what you were up to. I now see that you've been productive. Look what you've accomplished already! Enough pancakes to feed an army. What are you making tomorrow?"

"Ha, ha," she said but even her father's good-natured ribbing didn't bring Abe out of her funk.

"How was the pizza party last night?" Mrs. Gibson asked.

"Good."

"Did you meet the man of mystery?"

"Jack?"

"That's the one."

"Yes," Abe said. "I met him."

"Was he dreamy?" Mr. Gibson asked.

"Dad!"

"Stop teasing the girl, Bob," Mrs. Gibson said. "You're going to make her clam up and then we won't hear all the juicy details."

"There are no juicy details," Abe said. "It's all pretty boring really. Jack's originally from Chapel Hill but moved to Seattle after high school to go to the University of Washington. He graduated and found a job at IBM. He recently transferred to their office in Raleigh and moved back here. That's it for the juicy details."

"Oh," Mrs. Gibson said, disappointed. "That wasn't juicy at all."

"Yeah," Mr. Gibson added. "Your mother was hoping for more of a Cinderella-type story. You know, he sees you from across the crowded room; your eyes meet and you take one look at each other and are immediately swept away with a passionate, all-consuming love."

"That's precisely what I was hoping for," Mrs. Gibson said.

"Just like when we met, right Jan?" Mr. Gibson said, giving his wife a wink.

"I despised you at first, dear," Mrs. Gibson said sweetly. "Don't you remember? You were as skinny as a rail, and you used to whistle that stupid song everywhere you went. You were dreadfully annoying. Everyone said so."

"Hmpf," he snorted, picking up the newspaper.

"You did eventually grow on me," she added. "Although I don't recall when."

"It was at the prom. You were there with that hooligan, Kevin McCall. He took off with your best friend that night. I stepped in like the white knight that I am."

"Oh, yes," Mrs. Gibson nodded. "Kevin and Marsha lasted about a month after that, if my memory serves me. And you only danced with me because I asked you to. I was trying to annoy Marsha but my plan backfired. You danced like a walrus."

"That's not how I remember that night," he said, almost wistfully. "And I believe that was the night I swept you off your feet, right?"

"Yes," Mrs. Gibson said. "But it wasn't your dancing that did it. You stepped on my toes a few times and I don't know about you sweeping me off my feet. It was more of a nudge than anything else."

"So I nudged you off your feet then, did I?"

"Yes, so to speak, you did. At least it was enough of a push that I agreed to go to the movies with you the next night."

Abe listened to her parents' conversation and watched them as they talked. Mr. Gibson's eyes grew soft as he looked at his wife of twenty-eight years. "I fell in love with you at that movie," he said.

"And I fell in love with you."

"Yuck!" Abe exclaimed. She always felt gooey inside when she saw her parents look at each other that way. It was as if her parents were young lovers again—a thought that is horrifying to most normal offspring. "Stop with the mushy stuff already! It's seven o'clock in the morning for Pete's sake!"

"Would you prefer that your parents dislike each other?" Mr. Gibson asked. "I was merely reminding your mother of what a fine Prince Charming I was back in my day."

"Yucky!" Abe said, her eyes wide in horror.

"What's so yucky?" Mrs. Gibson said. "It was actually quite nice."

"Yes," Mr. Gibson added. "Don't you want a Cinderella–Prince Charming moment of your own?

Abe gasped, "Sorry to disappoint you, Dad, but there weren't any Prince Charming–Cinderella moments for me last night. And aren't you the one who threatened to pummel my last boyfriend."

"Wes?" Mr. Gibson said the word with utter disdain, and the mere act of uttering the dreaded name made his eyes flash with a deep, dark fury.

"Yes, Wes."

"He's lucky to be alive," Mr. Gibson said indignantly. "I never liked that boy. Was *he* there last night?"

"Yes, he was."

"How'd that go?" Mrs. Gibson asked.

"Fine," Abe said, shortly. "He was a perfect gentleman."

"Gentlemen do not behave the way that young man did," Mr. Gibson said, his voice dropping dangerously low.

"Dad, I know Wes was hardly wonderful, but you didn't make things any easier for him."

"What do you mean by that?"

Abe looked at her father in disbelief. Mr. Gibson's reputation for being somewhat assertive toward his daughter's dates was legendary. He'd sent more than one young man fleeing from the house. It was his custom to interrogate Abe's dates with all the warmth and good humor of a rottweiler in a junkyard. If, God forbid, one of the young men kept his daughter out later than instructed or committed some other infraction against his clearly outlined instructions—no matter how small or insignificant—Mr. Gibson would have a talk with the offender. Said talk would serve to enlighten the young man on just which rule was broken and to inform him that further violations would not be tolerated. Wes, in particular, endured Abe's father's disdain more than anyone else.

"Dad, you weren't nice to Wes," Abe said.

"I was nice to him. I said hello a couple of times, didn't I?"

"While you glared at him."

"Well, I was right about him, wasn't I? He wasn't good to you."

"Will Wes be at the barbecue tonight?" Mrs. Gibson asked.

"I could have a chat with him if you'd like, kiddo," Mr. Gibson told Abe. "I'll be sure to remind him that you are not a young woman who can be toyed with."

"Now, Bob," Mrs. Gibson warned. "You can't go around threatening people. Besides, if Abe is able to attend all of Megan's wedding events with a smile on her face, then why can't you?"

"I know, I know," Mr. Gibson said. "It's just that . . . I don't like that kid, Jan. I never did."

"We know, Dad," Abe said. "We know. You didn't like Wes. And you were right about him. He was a creep. Thanks for reminding me."

"Sorry," Mr. Gibson said. "Maybe next time you'll listen to your old man."

"Maybe," Abe said. "But Dad, Wes and I broke up six months ago. I've moved on. Now my best friend is getting married and I'm the maid of honor. There's going to be lots of parties where I'm going to see Wes, whether I like it or not. But I'm a big girl and I can handle it. I plan on being nice to everyone and smiling pretty in all the pictures. You should do the same."

"All right! All right! I'll be nice to Wes at the barbecue tonight. I'll even shake his hand if you want me to, but I'm only doing it for you and Megan."

"That's all I ask," Abe said. "And you don't have to worry about me spending any time with Wes whatsoever. Someone's called dibs on him."

"Dibs?" Mr. Gibson said. "I didn't know you girls did that sort of thing. That's barbaric."

"I thought so too, but Susie Keating did just that."

"Oh, Susie and Wes would look cute together," Mrs. Gibson said, but saw the expression on Abe's face and regretted it. "I'm sorry. I didn't know Susie was interested in Wes."

"She is, but she's equally interested in the new guy. She's taking Jack on a tour of Raleigh today." Abe's voice sounded biting even to her own ears, so she added a laugh at the end of the sentence in hopes of fooling her parents into thinking she didn't care who Susie Keating took on tours of Raleigh.

"I thought you said he was from Chapel Hill?" Abe's father asked. "Doesn't he already know his way around this town?"

"Yes," Abe said. "But he's been gone for a while, and Susie wanted him to feel welcome."

"That was nice," Mrs. Gibson said. "Then why did Susie call dibs on Wes if she's interested in the new guy?"

"I guess she wants to keep her options open, just in case she likes one of them more than the other."

"Barbaric!" Mr. Gibson said, shaking his head. "We

fellows are not toys to be used for your amusement, you know."

Abe shrugged. "You may be right, Dad, but I don't think these fellows mind it much. Personally, I think Susie's just on a manhunt."

"It sure sounds like it," he nodded. "It reminds me of when I was a young man. The women who stalked me . . . I can't tell you how bothersome it was."

"Yes," Mrs. Gibson said dryly. "Your father had to beat them back with a stick most days. It was dreadful. By the way, Abe, speaking of the barbecue, Dad and I are going to be a little late tonight getting to Megan's house. We're taking Aunt Maggie out to a late lunch."

"I thought you usually took Aunt Maggie out to lunch on Sundays?"

"We do," Mrs. Gibson hedged. "But . . ."

"You're both chicken!"

"No we aren't! That isn't it at all."

"Buck-buck-buck."

"I'm not chicken," she said. "It's just that . . ."

"It's just that, what?" Abe said, already knowing the answer.

"It's just that Linda Randal is a royal pain in the hind-end," her father said. "And we want to postpone . . . no savor . . . our awe of her party-planning skills for as long as we can."

"Oh, Dad," Abe sighed. "Megan's mom isn't that bad."

"She is that bad, and I'm merely stating a well-known fact. The woman's perfection is very annoying. She must be driving Megan crazy."

"Yes, she is, but it isn't anything Megan can't handle. Why not take Aunt Maggie to brunch instead? That way you'll get to the barbecue on time. I'm sure the food is going to be wonderful and the weather's been beautiful."

"Oh, all right," Mrs. Gibson sighed. "We'll eat like horses all day long. But would it have been too much to ask to have a thunderstorm ruin Linda's plans for a change? Nothing too upsetting for Megan, of course, just a little thunder and wind would be sufficient."

"Nope. That won't happen. Mrs. Randal has connections all the way to the top. It wouldn't dare rain today."

"I know," Abe's mother sighed. "Very well then, we'll arrive on time. At least, Dad and I can get a good look at this new fellow."

"Your mother will let me know if he's dreamy or not," Mr. Gibson added. "I'm not good at making those decisions."

Abe rolled her eyes. "First Megan, now you two! Why is everyone trying to play matchmaker?"

"We wouldn't do that," Mrs. Gibson said. "But if Susie Keating can call dibs, why can't you do the same?"

"Because Susie Keating is on a mission and I'm not. It's best that I stay out of her way."

"Hmpf," her father snorted. "Mission, smission. If she gives you any trouble tonight, I'd be happy to bump her into the swimming pool for you."

"Thanks," Abe said and smiled, only this time it was without effort. The image of Susie hitting the water was exactly what Abe needed to get her out of her bad mood.

Chapter Six

SATURDAY, JUNE 9

Abe was intentionally late getting to Megan's that afternoon. The thought of witnessing Susie's grand entrance with Jack was enough to make Abe stay home and watch television—not to mention Wes looking at Abe with puppy eyes every chance he got. She was startled by how quickly her heartache for him disappeared. Jack's arrival completely and totally dissolved those emotions. Now, suddenly, Wes was only someone she used to date. Good-looking, yes, but any spark that was once there was gone forever. So she arrived late to the barbecue, but only after she'd given herself a stern lecture about the downside of wishing Susie would fall into the pool.

As expected the weather was gorgeous. She dawdled on the Randals' front lawn so that she could allow herself a moment to enjoy the feel of the warm sun on her bare shoulders before she pushed open the gate to Megan's backyard. Abe wore a new sundress she'd bought especially for the occasion. She'd fallen in love with the dress as soon as she saw it on the hanger. It was a lovely floral print in pretty shades of plums and blues. It was far more expensive than anything else she'd purchased all year, but she couldn't resist. She liked the way the soft material fell around her legs and the colors were her favorites. She also liked the way it looked on her. She spent a long time getting ready that night, all the while telling herself that she was only fussing for Megan's sake. She'd even used the curling iron on her hair and it held, for once defying the North Carolina humidity, which continued to be unusually low for June.

"Abigail!" Megan shouted when Abe walked into the backyard, destroying all hopes for an inconspicuous arrival.

"Megan!" she shouted back. Abe smiled and greeted everyone as she made her way across the large patio that surrounded the swimming pool to get to Megan and Billy who were standing near the back door. Abe was her usual warm and friendly self; no one who saw her knew she was having a difficult day.

Megan gave her a big hug and handed her a pink drink with a purple flower floating on top. "I'm so glad you're here," she said, almost desperately. "My mom's been on a rampage." Megan looked beautiful. She was wearing a black wrap dress that showed off her shining hair and gorgeous tan.

"Thanks," Abe said, taking the drink. "I'm glad I'm here too. Do you want me to tackle her?"

"Not yet. I'll let you know."

"This is beautiful, Megan. Everything's perfect."

"Thank you. I had to fight my mom on the luau theme she wanted. Otherwise we all would have been standing here wearing grass skirts and watching a flamethrower. This is so much more tasteful, don't you think?"

"Absolutely."

"Where's Jack?" Megan asked, trying to look innocent.

"Jack?" Abe said, trying her best to look indifferent. "I don't know. I'm sure he and Susie will be along any minute now, or should I say Susan?"

"Susie? Why would Jack be coming with Susie?"

Abe explained the tour of Raleigh that Susie was leading and was surprised when Megan's cheeks flushed to a shade of bright pink. "That . . . that brat!" she said, exasperated. "I thought Susie called dibs on Wes!"

"She called dibs on everyone, remember? And why should you mind if she shows Jack around?"

"No!" Megan said, loud enough for Billy to look over at her from across the patio. "No. No. No! Susie's just being greedy now. She called dibs on Wes! I mean, dibs is dibs, right? When a person calls dibs, shouldn't it mean that that person wants dibs? You can't just call dibs on everyone! That isn't fair!"

Abe tilted her head and looked at her friend. Megan's hands were on her hips and her head jerked from side to side when she talked, as it often did when she was annoyed with something. "What difference does it make?" Abe asked. "Susie can give Jack a tour of Raleigh. I'm sure it's completely innocent." Of course Abe couldn't tell Megan that she was just as annoyed with Susie. Maybe even more so. Instead Abe tried to make her point. "Megan, are you still trying to fix me up with Jack?" she asked. "Because I thought we agreed that I wouldn't be going on any more of your blind dates?"

"Jack isn't a blind date," she said. "You've seen him already. It's only a blind date if you haven't seen him, Abe. That's why it's called a "blind" date. I thought you knew that. Now it's called a fix up."

"You're still playing matchmaker," Abe grumbled. "Stop it, Megan."

"But Jack's perfect for you. And he's such a good friend of Billy's. It would be so great if . . ."

"It's too late," Abe said, forcing herself to smile. "Susie called dibs. Besides, Jack is on to you. He knows you and Billy are trying to set us up. Stop it or I'll pinch you, bride or not."

Megan tossed her long hair off her shoulder and gazed steadily at Abe. "Okay," she groaned. "You're right. I'm obnoxious. I'll stop. I made the introduction, right? Now I just need to let nature take its course . . . and it would, too. If only everyone else would just cooperate! Susie is such a . . ."

"Let's get you married first," Abe said. "Then we'll worry about my love life. Deal?"

"All right," Megan said, still looking steamed. "It's a deal."

"Hey," Billy said, sliding up next to them. "Don't look now, but here comes Susie, Wes, *and* Jack."

"What!" Megan said, unable to hide the shocked expression on her face. "Isn't that cozy?"

Susie stepped onto the patio with Wes on one side and Jack on the other.

"Uh-oh," Billy said with a perplexed look on his face. "This could get a whole lot weirder." Megan and Abe followed his gaze and both instantly saw the reason for his outburst. Susie was walking toward them wearing an expensive floral sundress in dazzling shades of plum and blue. Abe's mouth dropped open. Susie was wearing the same exact dress as the one she was wearing! Susie looked at Abe with an annoyed, tight-lipped expression on her face as she walked toward them.

Abe threw back her head and roared with laughter. "I like your dress!" she howled as the trio approached.

"I like yours too," Susie said, looking not nearly as amused.

"Miss Louisa's House of Fashion, right?"

"Right."

Jack and Wes were now smiling too. "Great minds think alike, I guess," Wes said. "You both look very pretty."

"Thanks," Abe said, still smiling.

"Thank you," Susie said and beamed.

A thought flashed in Abe's mind and she instantly knew that Susie was thinking the same thing—was it her imagination or did Susie look better in the dress than Abe did? It was clear from the expression on Susie's face what she thought the answer to that question was.

Susie was curvier than Abe and the plums and blues went well with her dark hair and porcelain skin. The dress seemed to have a little more flounce to it too, mostly because Susie seemed to fill it better.

Abe shrugged it off. It wasn't Susie's fault that the dress looked perfect on her. Everything looked perfect on Susie. Instead she gave Susie a warm hug. "You look beautiful," she laughed. "I love your dress!" A statement she meant from the bottom of her heart.

Megan smiled broadly at Abe. Crisis averted, her eyes seemed to say. "Thanks," she whispered. "I owe you one." She then launched into an animated conversation about their plans for the night. Abe didn't know how long they'd stood there, the six of them, laughing and talking. All she knew was that she was doing everything in her power not to melt to butter because Jack was standing next to her. Fortunately, a man in a chef's hat and a white smock walked onto the center of the patio and announced that the buffet was ready. Abe was relieved that the swooning feeling she felt the night before had subsided. Of course, she was careful to not actually look at Jack. It was enough to know that he was next to her only inches away. That fact only made her knees wobble.

Abe decided she couldn't very well stand there and not talk to him though, so she listened with apt concentration to every word Megan was saying, pretending that she was totally engrossed in what she was saying. The group continued to stand and talk for a long time, graciously waiting for the rest of the guests to partake from the lavish buffet. Billy's arm was around Megan's waist, and Abe noticed that Wes's hand rested on the small of Susie's back. Jack stood next to Abe and it was all she could do to not to fall against him.

"You handle yourself well," he whispered in her ear while the others were in deep conversation.

"Thanks," she said, allowing herself to steal a glance at him and smile.

"Most women would have had a fit if that happened to them," he said. "You just laughed it off. You've got a great sense of humor."

"Laughed off what?" she said. "Oh, the dress? *Pffft.* That's no biggie. Life's too short to have a fit over something like that."

"I agree with you. But not everyone would have handled it as well as you did."

"Thank you."

Their eyes met once again, and immediately Abe felt that same stomach-churning, rubbery-kneed feeling she felt every time she looked at him. "How was your tour?" she asked, swallowing the hard lump in her throat.

"It was fun," he shrugged. "We just drove around for a half hour. Then we picked up Wes."

Abe's heart skipped a beat. They picked up Wes? Somehow that news made her feel deliriously happy. "Oh?"

"Yeah, Susie said he wanted to tag along."

"Hey," Megan said, interrupting Abe's joy. "Let's eat already. I'm starving."

The group began to drift toward the buffet table. Wes led Susie by the hand, making certain that they were several feet away from the others. Then Billy followed behind with Megan. "Shall we?" Jack asked, offering his hand.

"Yes," Abe said, taking it. "We shall."

The buffet table was full of mouthwatering food. There were two types of barbecue, beef and pork, along with several salads and an assortment of side dishes, including Abe's favorite, stuffed mushrooms. Everything looked delicious and the guests loaded up their plates while soft music played in the background.

Megan and Billy headed to the table where Billy's family was sitting, and Wes and Susie wandered to a vacant table on the far side of the patio. "Those two look like they want to be alone," Jack said. There was a slight edge in his voice. "Why don't you and I sit over there with the whole gang?" he said, pointing to the table where all their friends were sitting. Kasey, Andrew, Chandler, Sean, Taylor, and George were already sitting down and eating.

"Okay."

"Nice dress!" Sean shot when they sat down.

"Yeah," Kasey said. "Did you two plan to look like twins?"

"You're hotter," George said, sincerity dripping from every word.

"He told Susie the same thing five minutes ago," Andrew said, taking pleasure in ratting out his friend.

"I was just saying that to make her feel good," George said. "Abigail is much hotter in that dress than Susie."

"Yeah," Andrew said. "You're much hotter, Abigail."

"Thanks for your votes, guys," Abe said.

The next hour was a blur of good food and drinks and conversation for Abe, along with the thrill of having Jack so close. After dinner several of the guests began dancing. Jack and Abe watched from their chairs, content to just sit side by side.

"Hello, gorgeous," a familiar voice said. She looked and saw her father standing behind her.

"Hello there, handsome," Abe said. "And you too, madam. What a lovely couple you two make."

"Thank you," her mother said. "Is everyone having fun? Hi, kids."

The table greeted Abe's parents warmly. Everyone there knew them very well. "These people aren't my parents," Abe told Jack. "But I'll introduce you anyway. This is Bob and Jan Gibson. Mr. and Mrs. Gibson, this is Jack."

"Nice to meet you, Jack," Mrs. Gibson said. For some reason, Abe's father was tardy in displaying his usual hostility toward any male who dared stand next to his daughter. It was a favor that he'd never extended to anyone before.

"Nice to meet you, sir," Jack said, standing and shaking his hand, oblivious to the possible danger.

"I understand you've recently returned to the area," Abe's father said. "It's good to know that Raleigh's such a desirable place to live."

"I'm glad to be back."

"What line of work are you in, son?" Mr. Gibson asked.

"I'm a CPA with IBM."

"No kidding? My daughter's an accountant too."

"He knows, Dad," Abe said, looking at Jack warily. Instead of assaulting him, however, Mr. Gibson began talking to him about the tax code, a subject Abe avoided at all costs. Clearly her father didn't see this newcomer as much of a threat. Odd behavior, but Abe was relieved her father wasn't scowling at him.

"Hey, Mr. Gibson," Erin called from a table near the patio. "Aren't they playing your song?"

Mr. Gibson perked up his ears and listened. Sure enough, Toby Keith was singing in the background. "You're right," he said, his eyes lighting up. He then grabbed Abe's hand. "Come on, cupcake, dance with your old man."

"Charmed," she said, laughing. She waved a quick good-bye to Jack as her father pulled her toward the patio/dance floor. Several people got up from various tables around the patio and followed behind them, watching hopefully with amused eyes. Mr. Gibson then led Abe in a herky-jerky dance, if you could call it that. It was actually more of a twitch than a dance and the watchers began to cheer with approval, their deepest wish having been granted. They were going to witness one of the funniest sights that Raleigh had to offer— Bob Gibson dancing. It was common knowledge that Abe's father was a horrible, horrible dancer.

Abe followed along as best she could. "Take it easy

this time, Dad," Abe told him. "We've talked about this before, haven't we?"

"I'll behave myself. I've got it under control."

"You better!" Abe warned.

"Don't I always?"

"No."

"I saw your friend."

"What friend is that? I have several."

"Wes," her father said, wrinkling his nose.

"Uh-oh," Abe said. "Dad, didn't we talk about this?"

"I'll have you know I greeted him politely and didn't threaten him once."

"That's nice, Dad. Keep it up. I'm glad you're controlling yourself."

"I try," he said and stepped on her toe. "Sorry, cutie. I just keep reminding myself that Wes is some other father's problem now. I like that other one."

"Careful, Dad!" Abe said, as her father painfully poked her with a flailing elbow. "What other one?"

"That other boy," her father said. "Jack. I like him. He seems to have a lot on the ball."

"That's nice," Abe said. "But you just met him, Dad."

"I still like him."

"I'm glad you refrained from being mean to him. What's gotten into you?"

"Thank you. I told you I was behaving myself. So?"

"So, what?"

"So what do you think of this new fellow?"

"He's nice."

"Do you like him?"

"Sure. Sure, I like Jack. What's not to like?"

"Come on, Abe," Mr. Gibson groaned. "I saw you talking to him. He likes you. I can tell by the way he looks at you. And I get the feeling you might like him too." Mr. Gibson ended the sentence with a mighty spin that almost knocked her over. Fortunately, the next song was a slow one. Mr. Gibson's slow dance was not nearly as hideous as his fast steps.

"I was just being polite, Dad," Abe said, trying to lead. "Jack's a nice guy."

"You really know how to rake these poor boys over the coals don't you, Abe? You must get that from your mother."

"What do you mean?"

Her father shook her head. "My dear daughter, men don't want to be thought of as 'nice guys.'"

"What's wrong with being thought of as a nice guy?"

"What happens to nice guys, Abe?"

"I don't know. Nothing?"

"Come on, you know, nice guys . . ."

"Nice guys, what?"

"They finish last," he said, trying to spin her. "Nice guys finish last!"

"That's silly, Dad. And it's not true. Nice guys are nice guys. Sometimes they finish last. Sometimes they finish first."

"It isn't silly, Abe. Trust me. I'm old, but I have fond memories. Men want to be thought more of as swashbucklers, pirates, cowboys . . . even gangsters! They don't want to be thought of as nice guys. And why is that?"

Abe looked up at her father doubtfully. "Because nice guys finish last?"

"Exact-a-mundo! To a man courting a woman, 'nice guy' is the second worst label to have stamped on your forehead."

"Well, Dad, we're not exactly courting. I don't even think people actually use that word anymore. What's the worst label?" Abe was still trying to keep in step with her father's dance moves, an effort that was impossible because the dance had absolutely no rhyme or reason.

"That would be 'friend.' "

Abe laughed. "I get your point, Dad, but I know you. If you thought that Jack was interested in me, you'd be snarling at him like a pit bull."

"Me?"

"Yes, you."

"I'd never do any such thing, Abe. What do you think I am, some kind of crazed father?"

"Yep. That about sums it up."

"I'm just looking out for you. It's kind of my job."

"I know," Abe said and gave her father a peck on the cheek. "But I barely know Jack. I just met him yesterday."

Mr. Gibson shrugged. "I understand. I just wanted you to know where I stood with respect to my position—just in case it becomes an issue some time in the near future."

"Noted," Abe said.

"I also see that Susan Keating is currently busy with Wes—leaving the playing field wide open. Why a pretty girl like her would give that moron the time of day is beyond me, but that isn't for me to say. Either way, that leaves Jack all by himself."

"He's sitting with a dozen people."

"I know. But you could still make a move on him now, if you wanted to."

"I think you've been spending too much time with Megan," Abe said, but her father only laughed and began a strange new dance that was a combination of the swim and the pony.

"Cut it out, Dad! You look like you're having a seizure!"

"I am having a seizure," he said, adding a leap and a twirl.

Abe couldn't help it, she started laughing. Peals and peals of laughter—so hard her belly began to hurt. She would have lain on the dance floor doubled over with laughter if it hadn't been for the ice-cold angry look that Mrs. Randal was now directing toward them. Abe tried to stop laughing, really she did, but she just couldn't.

Suddenly, Megan was there with them, bopping to the music and imitating Mr. Gibson's terrible dance, step by step. This only caused Abe to laugh even harder. It also brought other guests onto the makeshift dance floor—all swaying to the same bad steps. Bit by bit the guests drifted onto the floor, jerking and jumping and twitching. Even Mrs. Randal joined in, although she was a little stiff at first. Soon enough, though, she too was waving her arms and holding her nose and shimmying up and down with the rest of them.

Susie joined in too, but she made the silly dance look as graceful as a ballet. Wes was at her side, dancing along and staying as far from Mr. Gibson as he possibly could. When the song ended, the dancers were enjoying themselves too much to go back to their seats. Instead they continued dancing—everyone, that is, except for Abe who was able to escape from her father's clutches when her mother appeared.

"May I cut in?" Mrs. Gibson whispered.

"Oh, would you please?" Abe whispered back.

"Let me handle this," Mrs. Gibson said, and began dancing with her husband. Soon she'd managed to bring his dancing to a much calmer, slower step that was somewhat more pleasing to the eye, but not much.

Abe made her way back to the table and sat down in a chair. She was flushed and tired from dancing, and she'd lost track of where her friends were.

"Don't stop now, Abigail," she heard a voice say. She looked up and saw Jack sitting alone at the other side of the table. He picked up his glass and moved over to sit next to her. "I was enjoying watching you and your father dance."

Abe smiled. "He's not my father. I've never seen that man before in my life."

"Really, because you have the same hair color."

"Coincidence."

"And the same natural sense of rhythm."

"Hey! That's not nice."

"Sorry," he said. "Can I get you a drink?"

"No, thanks. I still have some pink stuff in my glass."

They talked pleasantly and watched the crowd on the

dance floor. The music was playing and the people were dancing, calmer now but still going strong. Abe watched as her father took hold of her mother's waist and began an impromptu conga line that he led around the patio.

"Look what your father started," Jack said, laughing. "Is he always like this?"

"I wouldn't know," Abe said, blinking innocently. "I told you, I've never seen that man before in my life."

"Let's go sit under that tree," Jack said, suddenly taking her hand.

"Okay." She followed him to a stone bench that was situated under a magnolia tree in the corner of the Randal's backyard. It was somewhat cooler there, and Abe felt sudden goosebumps on her arms.

"It's quieter here," Jack said, pulling her down on the bench. "I was hoping I could get the chance to talk to you alone. It seems like you and I have a lot in common. I'd like to get to know you better."

Abe felt a thrill at the sound of his words, even though it was almost as if he was saying them in a dream. She was too busy drinking in the sight of him for the words to register—his warm brown eyes, the deep dimples. She shivered.

"Are you cold?" he asked.

"No. I'm fine," she said, her voice a whisper. He was looking into her face, his smile was soft and warm, and his hand was resting on her arm. Their eyes locked and, for a moment, Abe thought he was going to kiss her. She closed her eyes and leaned against him.

"Oh, no you don't!" Mrs. Randal shrieked, coming

toward them full speed ahead. "I want everyone dancing!" she ordered. "Especially the maid of honor and
the best man! Come on, you two. Get back to the patio
right this minute!"

Jack and Abe tried passive resistance to avoid Mrs.
Randal but that proved fruitless. Linda Randal was not
a woman who took no for an answer. Ever. Moments
later, Jack and Abe were back on the crowded patio,
getting bounced and shoved around by the throng of
gyrating people.

"This is so much better," Jack grimaced. "Maybe we
can try to slip away again as soon as she looks the
other way."

"Okay," Abe said, and boldly slipped her hand into his.

The conga line was still going strong. In fact, now it
was too large to be contained inside the patio and was
beginning to spill over to the area around the buffet
table. It snaked around the people who were going back
to the buffet table for seconds and continued around the
tables and chairs that were on the grassy lawn. When it
passed by them, Abe suddenly felt herself being yanked
into them.

"Come on!" Megan shouted, releasing Billy's waist
long enough to grab hold of Abe's wrist with one hand
and Jack's with the other. "Get in here!"

The next thing they knew, Abe and Jack were congaing across the yard with the rest of them. Abe
grabbed hold of Megan's back, and Jack slipped his
hands lightly onto hers. "Here we go!" he laughed.

The line of people snaked around the patio again.
Everyone was dancing and laughing and what few peo-

ple were left at the tables were soon pulled into the fray. Quickly the line was so long it had to loop around itself again and again, like a crooked, gyrating bull's-eye.

Mr. Gibson was at the head of the line, leading the way. Several people down were Wes leading Susie, followed by Taylor, Chandler, Kasey, Erin, and Derek. Suddenly Wes made a sudden break and turned the conga line into a new direction that moved toward the swimming pool. Dancing and rocking to the music, the new line twisted around the diving board and then down along the length of the pool. Just then the music changed to a disco song, and Wes suddenly stopped the line and broke into a wild, twirling dance. Other people followed suit and soon the conga line was breaking apart. People were crowded around the pool, some were still congaing, and some were disco dancing. "Wahoo!" Wes shrieked, grabbing Susie by the hand and spinning her. Abe felt Jack's hands tighten around her waist as Susie came dangerously close to bumping into them.

"Be careful," Jack said, pulling her toward him. "Someone's going to fall into the pool."

"I'm trying," Abe laughed back at him. The dancing continued until the next song which was a '50s number. Naturally the dancers began to do, what else, the twist. They crowded around the sides of the pool and spilled over onto the grass. Soon Wes and Susie's twist turned into a modified jitterbug, complete with spins and dips. Abe stepped back and avoided yet another near-miss with Susie.

"I'm getting you away from here," Jack said, taking

her by the elbow and pointing her toward the relative calm of the yard.

"Wait!" Susie shouted. "Don't go, Jack. The fun's just getting started. Dance with me!" She was laughing and dancing as Wes twirled and twisted and yanked her to and fro.

"I'll come back when it's safe, Susan," Jack promised, again trying to steer Abe away. They'd taken two more steps when Wes did a particularly dramatic dance move. He scooped Susie close to him, dipped her, hoisted her back up, then took her by the arm and swung her out again. The entire maneuver lasted only two seconds, but Susie was moving very quickly by the time it was done. Wes flung her away from him again, but just as her body reached as far as it could go, he lost his grip on her hand.

Susie was going too fast to catch herself, and she bumped into Jack and Abe with a force that was surprising for such a small woman. She was moving so quickly, it felt as if they'd been hit by someone much larger. Jack absorbed most of the impact, but not enough to keep Abe from getting smacked by Susie's shoulder. She jumped back sideways in a desperate attempt to avoid the collision—a move which immediately turned into a bad idea. For Abe there was a blinding second of uncertainty, then a peculiar sensation that the ground wasn't where it was supposed to be. For a second, she thought she would catch herself and be on solid footing, or maybe Jack's frantic grasp would somehow stop her before it was too late. But that hope was gone in an instant, and Abe knew what was going to happen next: There was a loud splash and then the touch and taste of cool water was all around her.

For a moment, Abe stayed underneath the surface, toying with the idea of swimming to the deep end and drowning herself before anyone noticed her. It seemed like a better alternative than sputtering up to the surface in her ruined dress and high heels. She looked around the bottom of the pool, hoping against hope that she'd find a forgotten snorkel so she could breathe into it until the crowd disbursed. Of course there was nothing there. Abe's chance for a graceful way out of her predicament quickly dwindled down to only one option. With nothing left to do, she adjusted her ballooning dress as best she could and floated to the top.

"OH MY GOSH!" Susie was shrieking. "I'm sooooo sorry! I'm SOOOOO SORRY! I didn't mean it. I swear I didn't mean it!"

Megan was shouting, and Wes was smirking. Abe wanted to sink back under the water again, but instead she laughed and did a backstroke around the perimeter of the pool. Why not? It was obvious that she'd fallen in. There was no getting around that embarrassing fact, and Abe decided to make the most of the situation. Jack was already at the ladder ready to jump in after her when she swam toward him.

"OH MY GOODNESS!" Susie was shouting. "OH MY GOSH! I'M SOOOOO SORRY!"

"It's okay," Abe said, flinging her wet hair out of her face as she climbed up the shaky ladder. But it wasn't okay. Her face was burning with red hot embarrassment and, more than anything else, she wanted to crawl underneath a table.

"Oops," Wes said, handing Abe a towel someone retrieved from the house. "I'm sorry Ab . . . Abigail."

Abe bit her tongue to keep from screaming at him. *Was he always such an idiot?* she wondered while she dried herself off with the towel.

"Wow," Wes said. He was suddenly staring at her; his usual smirk was replaced by another expression. An expression that Abe didn't readily recognize.

Abe gaped at him, bewildered. Why was he looking at her like that? Wes's eyes were moving up and down the length of her body. "You look . . . really, really good," he said.

"Shut up, you moron," Jack snapped, taking the towel from Abe and wrapping it around her shoulders protectively. "Here," he said, putting his arm around her and steering her towards the house. "Let's get you dried off." It was then that Abe realized her dress—her new pretty purple sundress—was clinging to her like a second skin, leaving very little to the imagination. She pulled the towel around her tighter while Jack hustled her past Wes, Susie, Megan, and her parents.

"Abigail?" he said from the outside of the bathroom door a few minutes later. "I found a robe you can use." Abe opened the door a crack, and Jack shoved in Mrs. Randal's fluffy neon orange bathrobe—the one with the big pink flamingos wearing turquoise sunglasses on the two front pockets.

"Thanks," Abe said. "This will do until I can raid

Megan's closet." She'd taken off her drenched dress and hung it over the towel bar. She was shivering and goosebumped when she pulled on the robe and peeked out the door. He was waiting for her, looking concerned. "Is it safe to come out?" she asked.

"Yes," he said. She walked out of the bathroom, almost swallowed up by the bathrobe.

Abe looked at him again and felt her face redden. "Thanks for getting me out of there," she said, knowing her cheeks were as pink as the flamingo appliqués on the pockets.

"No problem," Jack said. "That idiot Wes! Would you like me to toss him into the deep end for you? He's always been a moron. I'd be honored to drown him for you."

Abe smiled. "Maybe later. First I'm going to see if I can find something to wear in Megan's closet. Maybe I can still salvage some of my dignity." She ran up the steps, totally humiliated.

It wasn't that she'd fallen into the swimming pool; that sort of thing still occurred with alarming frequency during backyard parties amongst her friends. But she was usually better prepared. This was a more formal event and she hadn't thought to wear her swimsuit underneath her dress or to bring a spare set of clothes. Abe's face burned thinking about the way Wes had looked at her—and the way Jack had shouted at him. She thought he was going to punch Wes in the nose, and the intensity of his outrage matched the intensity of Abe's embarrassment. Somehow it made her melt inside again.

She shut and locked the door of Megan's bathroom and turned on the water for a shower. Ten minutes later she was out of the bathroom and pulling on a pair of well-worn blue jeans and an old shirt she found in Megan's dresser. The pants were too short and hung a little low at the hips but they would have to do. Abe combed her wet hair and borrowed some of Megan's makeup for a quick touch up. "Better," she said aloud, then opened the bedroom door. So much for spending hours getting ready for the evening.

She was surprised to find Jack sitting at the top of the staircase waiting for her. "Hi," he said. "You look great."

"I look like a wet rat."

"Yes, but a great looking wet rat," he said, and Abe broke into a smile. "We don't have to go back out there, you know," he said, suddenly taking her into his arms. "We can sneak out the front if you want. No one will ever see us. As a matter of fact, that would probably be more fun."

It was tempting. She buried her face against his shoulder and melted into his embrace. But Abe knew the party was outside, and as much as she hated the idea of facing everyone, she knew it was better if she did. "It's okay," she said. "I'll laugh about this in a week."

Jack gazed into her face, his eyes were shining and his arms were wrapped around her, holding her tightly. He was deliciously close. "I bet you will," he said. "Not only do you have a great sense of humor, you don't let things get you down. And you're not a drama queen either. Come on, wet rat; let's go show them what you're made of."

They walked back outside together, his hand holding hers protectively, as if he was going to do battle with anyone who teased her about her wet hair. As soon as they walked through the double French doors onto the patio, the partygoers erupted in applause and catcalls.

"Way to go!"

"Klutz!"

Abe curtsied, laughed, and high-fived her way through the crowd of people as Jack followed behind her. She even managed to fake punch Wes on the arm and then gave him a forgiving hug.

Chapter Seven

SUNDAY, JUNE 10

Everything was all set. Erin and Abe began working on their task first thing that morning. They worked efficiently and with little conversation other than their usual friendly banter. There was no need for conversation because they both knew what to do. The preparation of the food had been going on for days and included not only the efforts of Erin and Abe but also a baker and a deli, not to mention Mrs. Gibson. It was laid out in a mouth-watering display across two wooden picnic tables that were covered with lavender-checkered tablecloths. A vase of fresh-cut flowers anchored the end of each table. There were trays of cold cuts along with baskets of rolls and muffins. There were platters of chopped vegetables, cheeses, and chilled fruits. There was potato salad and chilled pasta salads, as well as a steaming Crockpot of meatballs and jambalaya. To drink there was a big bowl of sangria punch and, of course, several frosty pitchers of sweet tea. Bottles of beer and sodas were stocked in ice-filled tubs that were strategically placed around the patio. There were balloons in the wedding colors of lavender, fuchsia, and white tied to the chairs, light fixtures, and branches of the trees. A soft breeze helped cool the warm Carolina sun. Thankfully, it was going to be another picture-perfect day.

"This looks fantastic," Mrs. Gibson said as she walked outside, the screen door slamming behind her with a noisy bang. "You ladies have done a great job."

"Thanks," Erin said. "The guests should be here any minute."

"Thanks, Mom," Abe echoed. "I hope nothing goes wrong."

"It won't!" Erin smiled. "We've done too much work for anything to go wrong now. It's going to be perfect."

"Don't worry," Mrs. Gibson added. "This will be a wonderful wedding shower. Megan and Billy will love it. What could go wrong?"

"Ugh!" Abe groaned. "Don't ever use that expression again. Trust me, things can go wrong!"

"Don't worry about Susie," Erin said. "I'll keep an eye on her. Besides, you don't have a swimming pool."

Abe heard the doorbell ring through the screened patio door. She looked up at her mother and made a face of mock terror. "Here we go," she said and headed inside to greet her guests.

Fifteen minutes later things were going as smoothly as could be expected. Mr. Gibson was permitted to set up a boom box on the outskirts of the patio and was handling the music like a professional. He'd been given strict instructions on what to play (nothing fast enough to encourage conga lines) and, for reasons of public safety, he was forbidden to dance. Abe enacted this rule due to his culpability for the swimming pool incident. Logically, she knew that Wes was the one who'd spun Susie into her and caused her to topple over the side of the pool. But somehow she couldn't shake the notion that her father had ultimately started it all and was therefore at least partially to blame. She was thinking of keeping the dance ban until her own wedding.

The guests arrived in small groups of two or three until almost all of the invitees were there. Erin and Abe long ago gave up on the idea of a surprise party for the bride and groom. It was just too difficult a task to ask so many people to keep a secret.

Megan and Billy arrived promptly at the scheduled time. They were soon followed by several other couples, Kasey and Andrew, Taylor and George, Chandler and Sean, in an excited flurry. Derek helped out by making sure everyone had a cold drink in his or her hands. More friends arrived as did many of the honorees' family members. Mrs. Randal and Mrs. Meegan showed up together, hand in hand, twittering as if they'd known each other for decades. Finally, after what seemed like forever, Jack appeared. Abe was relieved to see that Susie was nowhere in sight.

"Hi," he said, and gave her a hug.

"Hi," she said. There was that dizzy feeling again, but she no longer tried to resist it. In fact, she enjoyed it.

"What can I do?" he asked, and immediately Mrs. Gibson seized the opportunity to send him to help Derek circle the area with trays of appetizers. Jack dove in to help, all too soon for Abe who would have preferred him to be closer. Much closer.

The patio quickly filled up. Erin, Derek, Abe, and Jack worked their way through the crowd and made sure that everyone had a cold drink or a snack. The weather was wonderful and the guests were enjoying themselves immensely. Abe surveyed the group with a critical eye. Everyone had a cup, a bottle, or a can and seemed to be enjoying themselves. The breeze was light but not strong enough to blow anything off the tables. Even the ice in the tubs behaved itself by not melting too quickly.

After the crowd was pleasantly situated, Abe made her first announcement. She told her guests that they'd have exactly ten minutes to tease her about her midnight swim the night before. After that, she declared firmly, all discussion on the subject would end and the bridal shower would proceed forward. To back up her position, she set a kitchen timer for exactly ten minutes and signaled when she was ready for the teasing to commence. The guests enthusiastically heckled her in catcalls and shouts, but Abe took it like a soldier. Jack stood next to her to ensure that they went easy on her, which they did. He only needed to glare at one or two people. When the timer went off, Abe held up her hands to indicate that their time was up and the teasing stopped immediately.

"Enough about me," she said. "This is Megan and

Billy's party. Let's have some fun!" And they did. First they played a game that Erin found in a party book. It involved asking the guests an assortment of questions about Megan and Billy's favorite things: colors, foods, sports, etc. Of course there were questions that no one knew the answers to: What was Billy's first pet? (A chocolate Lab named Bucky.) What is Megan's favorite holiday? (Christmas, not because of the presents but because she loves to decorate the tree.) Whoever answered the most questions correctly won a coffee cup with the grinning image of Megan and Billy stamped on it. Then they played a game similar to musical chairs called Who's Next? This game involved asking an equal number of male and female guests to stroll around the patio while scary, haunted house music played. Chairs had been lined up in two rows. One row had pink balloons attached to each chair, and the other row had blue balloons. Men circled the blue row and women circled the pink row. When Mr. Gibson flipped off the music, everyone lunged for a chair. There was always one less chair than people standing, and everyone was forced to scramble to find a seat. The last man to miss the chair with a blue balloon and the last woman who missed the chair with a pink balloon were "Next to Marry." Of course no one wanted to be sitting in the chairs with the balloons tied to them, and there was a lot of clambering and shrieking every time the music stopped. Caroline and Sean won, much to their horror. Fortunately for Abe, she was not required to play because she was an extra along with the married couples.

Afterwards, Erin invited everyone to eat. Abe was happy to see that the food was holding out well, although she and Jack needed to refill the tea pitchers and punch bowl several times. Another hour passed before Abe was able to look around the yard again. She smiled a satisfied smile. Everything went smoothly, perhaps even wonderfully. She was surprised that she didn't feel at all anxious about the party. Instead she felt relaxed. She was even enjoying herself.

"Hey girl," Megan said, sliding up next to her. "Thank you for the wedding shower. Everything is beautiful. I'm so touched I could cry."

"You're so worth it," Abe said, and gave her a hug.

"I'm sorry about last night," Megan said. "I'd really like to talk to you about it, if you have a minute?"

"Sure," Abe said. "You look as though something is bothering you."

"Something is bothering me," Megan said. She looked around to make sure no one else could hear them. It wasn't like Megan to gossip, but Abe sensed that she had something important to say that just couldn't wait. "I was so angry with Wes and Susie last night," Megan said. "They thought it was all so darn funny! Why did Wes have to move the conga line so close to the pool anyway? And Susie! Sheesh, what a klutz!"

"It was an accident," Abe said. The warm, sunny afternoon and the happy mood of the shower made her almost forget her humiliation from the night before.

"I know, but they should have been more careful. Can your dress be saved?"

"Yes. I took it to the dry cleaner this morning, and they said it would be good as new."

"That's a relief," Megan said.

"Forget about it," Abe told her.

"All right. But what if something like that happens on my wedding day?"

"Bite your tongue. Your wedding will be perfect. It's okay, Meg. There was no harm done. Not really. So I fell into the swimming pool. We both know I'm no stranger to embarrassing moments."

"Still, Susie Keating is a big dope, and I plan on having a long talk with her when I get back from my honeymoon. Did you see the way she was hanging all over Wes?"

"Well, she called dibs, didn't she?"

"Ugh!" Megan groaned. "That didn't stop her from hanging all over Jack too."

Abe felt a tug of worry. "She was?"

"Like tinsel on a Christmas tree," Megan's face was flushed. "But, Abe, what I wanted to tell you was this: It's obvious to everyone that Susie is flirting with Jack so that she can get Wes's attention. You do see that, don't you?"

"Maybe she is," Abe said, glancing across the patio at Susie. "And maybe she isn't. It doesn't matter. Susie is single. Besides, Megan, Wes and Jack are big boys and I don't think they mind it when Susie flirts with them."

"But Wes minds it when Susie flirts with Jack. Not that I don't enjoy seeing Wes squirm like a worm. Even still, I think Susie's a big flirt! It's as if she wants all the guys to herself! Can't she just latch onto Wes and stop bothering everyone else?"

Abe kept the smile pasted on her face and listened while Megan huffed and puffed. "Never mind the soap opera stuff," she said finally. "All you have to worry about right now is your wedding day."

"Yeah, well I may just blow up before then!" Megan said and, as if to accentuate her point, the sound of Susie's laughter came from across the patio. "You're so funny, Jack," she was saying, her voice high and giggly. Abe and Megan glanced up and saw Susie leaning close to him, looking pretty and tanned and fabulous in a white eyelet skirt and pink halter top. Susie looked up too and saw Abe and Megan watching her. She smiled and waved at them as she let her hand slip onto the top of Jack's arm.

"See what I mean?" Megan said, shooting Susie an angry glare. "Come on, Abe. Let's go over there and show her how it's done!"

"What? I have to pass around the—" It was too late. Megan grabbed Abe's arm and yanked her across the yard to where a group of people were standing. Susie was in the center of things, of course.

"Hi," Megan said. "Isn't this a wonderful shower?"

"Very nice," Wes said, looking cautiously at her. Abe had the distinct feeling that Megan addressed her dissatisfaction about the swimming pool incident to Wes earlier that day because now he was trying to keep himself as inconspicuous as possible. His hands were shoved in his front pockets and his shoulders were slouched down low. "I'm sorry about last night, Abigail," he said, looking at Abe with that puppy dog, sad expression that once made her heart jump.

"You should be," Susie cooed. "Boy, was Megan mad."

"I still am."

"I know you are. I'm soooo sorry, Abigail. Can you ever forgive us?" There was a coy lilt to Susie's voice and Abe fought the urge to tell her that she was soooo sick of her, but this was Megan and Billy's shower and Susie was her guest.

"Oh, Susie," she said. "Don't worry about it. It was an accident."

"I'm sooooo sorry," she said again.

"Me too," Wes said. "I'll have to make it up to you somehow."

He smiled at her sweetly. It was the same gorgeous smile that he used so well when they'd dated—the one that once made her feel weak in the knees. Only now, Abe found it to be insincere. But she also saw the look on Susie's face when Wes looked at her. It was an expression of masked panic, there and gone so quickly that Abe thought she'd imagined it. "You do owe me, don't you?" Abe said to him in her best teasing voice so she could test her theory.

"Absolutely," Wes said in a low, sexy voice. "And I'd do anything to make it up to you. Just say the word. I'm yours for anything you want. Anything at all."

She fought the urge to slap him, but she was enjoying the effect his words had over Susie. Abe hated to admit it, but seeing Susie's cheeks suddenly turn a soft shade of pink and her eyes grow as wide and round as saucers somehow pleased her.

"We should cut the cake now," Susie said, smiling a big, fake smile and looking at Abe with piercing hazel-green eyes.

"Okay," Abe said, giving her a triumphant smile of her own. "Let's do that."

Abe quickly decided Susie had had enough torture for one day. Also, flirting with Wes was making her feel squeamish, especially with Jack looking on. So she found Erin and together they called theirs guests around for the cake cutting and started handing out lavender paper plates and napkins. Abe was so busy passing out slices of cake that she didn't notice it when Jack was suddenly beside her. He smiled and took the knife she was holding out of her hand and placed it on the table. "You have enough cake set out to feed a battalion," he said. "Why don't you relax for a couple of minutes? Come and sit with me."

"Yeah," Erin said. "Go sit down and eat your cake, Abigail. I'll take it from here."

His invitation was music to her ears, and the butterflies in her stomach took flight again. He took her hand, and she followed him as he led her to the white wooden bench next to her mother's vegetable garden. She felt suddenly flushed as memories of sitting on a different bench with him came flooding back to her. It was then that Abe knew that he was going to kiss her. She could tell by the way he was looking at her with soft, warm brown eyes. The knowledge sent currents of thrilled electricity racing through her body.

They sat on the bench and looked at each other, smiling shyly. He was more handsome than she'd initially thought. The deep dimples were by far his best feature, but his eyes were nice too. He didn't have the rugged, sexy good looks that Wes possessed, but Abe now found him to be far more attractive. Jack had the kind of face she'd never get tired of. His face was friendlier and easier to look into than any other man she'd ever known. It was an uncomplicated kind of handsome. A nice guy handsome. Abe blinked a few times and cleared her throat, and wondered why it was suddenly so hot.

"I've never been to a wedding shower before," he said. "This is fun."

"Yes, it is. I'm glad you're enjoying yourself." Their eyes met and locked. Then he leaned in closer to her and kissed her, just like she knew he would. Finally. It was a kiss that happened as naturally as the sunrise, as if it was supposed to happen. His lips were warm and delicious and irresistible. His mouth opened slightly against hers and she melted into him, returning the kiss with a passion that surprised her. He lightly cupped his hand under her chin and pulled her closer to him. His tongue probed her mouth and she felt her insides catch on fire. It felt as if she'd never been kissed before. Abe let her hand slide to his waist and wrapped her arms around him and held him tight. It felt glorious being so close to him.

"Wow," she whispered, finally pulling away slowly.

"Wow," he whispered back. She pulled back just enough so they could breathe and they stared at each other, oblivious to everyone and everything around them. "Abigail," he began, his voice soft. "I've been trying to get you alone for a long time now and now that you're here, I don't know what to say. I . . ." Nothing else was said for a long moment. They just looked into each other's eyes.

"Ahem," a voice said from above. Abe reluctantly tore her gaze away from Jack's face and looked up. There was Susie standing in front of them, blocking the warm sunshine and smiling.

"Jack, I was hoping you and I could talk," she said, apologetic but determined. "I hope I'm not interrupting anything important."

"Uh . . . I . . ." he began. "Well . . ."

"If that's okay with you, Abigail," Susie said, glancing at Abe. Abe could tell from the expression on Susie's face that she hadn't seen them kissing. Surely if she did, she never would have approached them. But there she was, standing in front of them looking like she'd never leave.

"Um . . . okay. Sure," Abe stammered.

"Err . . ." Jack said.

"It's okay," Abe said, feeling her face redden. "I should get back to my guests." She was suddenly terribly embarrassed. What was she thinking? Sitting on a bench and kissing a man who was practically a stranger? At her own party yet! Abe hoped no one had seen them. Fumbling, she stood, smiled awkwardly at Susie and bolted back toward the patio. Once there, she grabbed an empty pitcher of sweet tea and took it to the kitchen for yet another refill. She returned to the party, smiling and chatting to the guests, hoping that her face wasn't as flushed as it felt. She poured tea into empty plastic cups as quickly and as furiously as she could, but every few minutes she found herself glancing toward the bench. Susie and Jack were in a deep discussion but their expressions gave her no insights as to what they were talking about. Susie's eyes were shining bright and she was sitting on the bench close to him, her hand resting lightly on his hand. He was listening intently and nodding. Abe wished she knew what they were saying.

"Do you think it's time to open presents?" Erin said, sliding up next to her.

"Sure. Let's round everyone up."

Abe gathered all her guests to the patio, although she didn't have the courage to interrupt Susie and Jack. Instead Mrs. Gibson collected them and brought them over to the tables on the patio.

The next hour went by quickly as Megan and Billy took turns opening the brightly wrapped boxes. Abe was forced to forget about Susie and Jack's private conversation because she was too busy with the chore of writing down an inventory of the gifts so that Megan and Billy could send thank-you notes later. But her mind kept drifting back to him. She could still taste his kiss on her lips. Why wouldn't he look at her?

"Ohhh," Megan said. "This is so beautiful."

"This is great," Billy said.

"I love it."

"We needed this desperately. Thank you so much."

"I've always wanted one of these. I'll treasure it."

One package after another was opened as Abe dutifully wrote down the details on a yellow legal pad. She couldn't help herself; in between each gift she found herself seeking out Jack. He'd joined the festivities but he was standing toward the back of the group next to Susie, quietly watching Megan. Abe wished he would look her way, if only to offer her a smile, but he didn't. She did, however, notice that Wes was watching Susie intently. She also noticed the expression on his face—it was a look that was a little baffled and a little angry.

He likes her. The thought popped into Abe's head, and she instantly knew it was true. Wes liked Susie in a way he'd never liked her. A week ago, that knowledge would have hurt her to the center of her being, but now she acknowledged the fact without any regret whatsoever. She no longer cared that she wasn't Wes's best girlfriend.

Abe watched Susie warily. She was smiling and talking to Jack, but occasionally she would glance fervently in Wes's direction. Once she even caught his eye. But that only lasted a second, then she tossed her hair back and leaned into Jack to whisper something in his ear. It seemed to Abe that Susie had made a choice between her two suitors. Unfortunately, she'd chosen Jack and that was Abe's first choice too.

"But why did you kiss me?" Abe wanted to shout at him. She'd felt so certain there was a spark between them—an electricity she'd felt with every beat of her heart every second she was near him. A connection that she now had to accept was only on her part because, now, Jack wouldn't even look at her.

Some spark, she thought to herself bitterly. Susie merely needed to crook her pretty little finger and Jack had forgotten all about the kiss they'd so recently shared. Abe's heart was breaking, but there was nothing she could do about it. She didn't know what the etiquette was in this sort of situation either. Was a hostess allowed to entertain a broken heart during the event? Probably not, Abe decided. This was Megan's wedding shower and she was the maid of honor. She'd have to put on a smile and pretend that she was happy with Jack's choice. Even if it was killing her.

So Abe did what she always did whenever she felt sad; she put a big smile on her face and tried to make the best of the situation. Anyone who saw her would have thought that she was the happiest person at the party, except she wasn't. She was the most miserable person at the party.

The presents were all opened, and the guests were running out of things to say. The party was finally winding down, and people began to say their good-byes. Abe felt both relieved and panicked at the same time.

"Where's Jack going with Susie?" Megan said to Kasey. She didn't see Abe who had crouched down to pick up a piece of cake before Bailey, the dog, spotted it.

"I don't know," Kasey said. "I thought she had a thing for Wes."

"That's news to me," Wes said, looking disgusted.

"But you were getting along so well last night," Megan said. "What happened?"

"Beats me," he said, trying to look as though he didn't care.

It was then that Megan noticed that Abe was still crouching near the table. "Abe!" she said, looking startled and guilty. "This was the most beautiful wedding shower ever. I can't thank you enough."

"No, thank you, good buddy," Abe said, and gave her a big hug. "This was so much fun!"

"Everything was perfect."

"Absolutely perfect," Kasey echoed.

"Wonderful."

"Gorgeous."

"I had a great time."

Abe noticed that Megan and Kasey were talking quickly, too quickly. And standing shoulder to shoulder, as if they were trying to block her view from something they didn't want her to see—a pointless endeavor since Abe was almost a half foot taller than they were and could easily look over their heads and see that Susie and Jack were leaving . . . together.

"Oh, we can't forget the hostess," Susie was saying as she pulled a reluctant Jack behind her. "Thank you so much, Abigail. Everything was beautiful."

Megan glared at Susie menacingly, but it was too late. Susie was a safe three feet away and holding onto Jack's arm with what appeared to be a death grip.

"It was great," Jack said, his eyes avoiding Abe. "Thanks . . . for everything."

"Thanks for coming," Abe said, the smile on her lips felt frozen and it was all she could do to keep herself from asking him not to go. But he was leaving and there was nothing she could do to stop him. He was leaving . . . with Susie.

"Where are you two going?" Kasey blurted, glaring at them crossly.

"Susan needs a ride home," Jack said, glancing back at Abe but as soon as she caught his eye, he looked down at his feet.

"The sun's going down," Susie said quickly, giving a

darting glance in Wes's direction. "And it's such a pretty night. It'll be a sunset drive."

Wes stared at her and shrugged. "Too bad he can't put the roof down," he said, knowing how much Susie liked his bright red convertible. She walked past him, tightly holding Jack's hand, ignoring the remark.

"Have fun," he said coolly.

Jack looked at Wes, obviously annoyed. "Will do," he said with an equal chill.

Susie smiled sweetly at Wes then wrapped her arm in Jack's. "See ya later," she said. "Thank you for a lovely party but we really do have to go." Her voice was light and sweet and she smiled at Wes with clear, bright eyes and an almost angelic smile. Then she led Jack away.

Chapter Eight

WEDNESDAY, JUNE 13

The next three days passed in a slow, creeping snail's pace. Abe jumped whenever the phone rang, even though she knew that Jack wasn't going to call. For all the other members of the bridal party, however, those same three days were a whirlwind of activity. They were so busy they barely had time to catch their collective breath, especially Megan. In addition to the barbecue the previous weekend and the Jack and Jill wedding shower, Abe and the bridesmaids made plans to take Megan out to dinner for one last night out with the girls. Of course it wouldn't really be their last night out but it would be Megan's last night out as a single woman. Come Saturday evening, she would become Mrs. William Meegan.

They chose The Raindrop Pub—better known as The Raindrop. It was their favorite pub, the one they went to when they watched football and basketball games and the one they went to when they wanted to have a loud, rocking good time. It was a rollicking place most of the time, more so than Mario's, but not so much that it ever got out of hand. The atmosphere was casual and relaxed. Not the kind of place for people who wanted to strike a pose of style and sophistication. It was more of a place to go just to have fun.

The Raindrop was decorated in warm colors of chocolate brown and sage green with the requisite dizzying array of sports memorabilia on the walls. There was a large bar that was dominated by two big screen televisions on each side making The Raindrop an ideal place for sports fans. A separate section of tables was placed on the other side of the restaurant for those patrons who preferred quieter, more private gatherings, although there was no lack of television sets there either.

Megan and her friends spent untold hours at The Raindrop during and since their college days, drinking many a pitcher of cold beer and eating potato skins and quesadillas. They were such regulars that most of the employees knew them by name. A few members of their gang even worked at The Raindrop at one time or another and now, after years of patronage, it was still their favorite hangout.

Abe dressed carefully. She wore a bouncy black skirt with a top that had a splashy black and hot pink print on it. She brushed her hair until it shined and wore it long down her back on the theory that should Susie have another accident, she could hide herself underneath it. She still felt her face flush when she thought back to the barbecue and the shower. She became even more flustered, however, when she thought about Jack and the way he kissed her and then left her without so much as a good-bye.

The thought of yet another evening spent in the company of Susie Keating bothered Abe enormously, although she would never have admitted it. She knew that she needed to conduct herself in a manner befitting a proper maid of honor. All things considered (and Abe suspected she was being childish), she was having trouble convincing herself that a night at The Raindrop would be the blast she pretended it would be.

Why did Susie have to sweep him away—just when things were becoming so promising? Abe could still taste Jack's kiss on her lips. In fact, all she had to do was close her eyes and she could almost relive it all over again. But then she remembered the way he wouldn't look at her when he left with Susie. He'd left with Susie! What more did Abe need before she faced the truth? Jack made his choice and it wasn't her. She reminded herself of that fact countless times and the stinging hurt never got any easier to take. She needed to get it through her head, once and for all, that Jack wasn't the nice guy she thought he was.

Abe's forehead furrowed in deep thought as she drove to the restaurant. Not even the music of Refreshments in the Lobby coming from her car CD player could erase the image of Jack and Susie walking away arm in arm. The thought made Abe ache with envy. How could he leave with Susie after he'd just kissed her? How could Susie be so quick to forget Wes? Of course, Wes did the same thing himself to far too many other women. Leave it to Susie to be the one to give Wes a taste of his own medicine.

Abe's first stop was Chandler's house. She pulled into the driveway and honked the horn twice. Then she drove the short block away to Taylor's house. As usual Taylor was late, but Chandler had already threatened her earlier so they only had to wait ten minutes.

"Finally!" Chandler scolded her as she piled into the car. Taylor's cheeks were flushed from rushing although she'd been getting ready for nearly two hours. She wore a bright orange T-shirt and a pair of crisp khaki capris, yet despite her cuteness, she still wore an air of someone who was rushed.

"Sorry," Taylor said. "George called. My hair isn't even dry."

Chandler shook her head in exasperation and gave Taylor a look of profound annoyance. "Hmpf," she snorted.

"Ladies," Abe said gently. "There will be no catfights tonight, remember? This is Megan's night."

"All right," Chandler agreed reluctantly, giving Taylor one last glare. "Where's everyone else?"

"We're going to pick up Kasey next. Susie, Kirsten, and Caroline are going to meet us there."

"What about Megan?" Taylor asked.

Megan? Abe felt a sudden panic. "Oh, no!" she gasped. "In all the excitement, I forgot to ask Megan if she needed a ride! Quick, Chandler, call her on your cell phone."

Chandler made the call as Abe turned the corner, too quickly. She was minutes from Kasey's apartment building but she was already calculating the route she would take when she backtracked to pick up Megan.

"It's okay," Chandler said. "Susie called her earlier. They're already in the car."

"Whew!" Abe sighed, although she wasn't pleased with herself for forgetting the bride. Some maid of honor she'd turned into. She was even less pleased that Susie was the one who picked up the slack. "This wedding is making me crazy," she confessed. "I love Megan, but I'll be glad when June 23rd gets here."

"Me too," Taylor said. "I'm going to dance all night long."

The restaurant was crowded but Abe made reservations well in advance. They were quickly seated at a big table in a separate dining room, far from the noisy bar area, and set up just for them. The long table was already bustling with laughing, noisy women.

"Hey!" Megan shouted. "'bout time you guys got here."

"Blame Taylor," Chandler groused.

"I was only a few minutes late!"

"Don't even say it!" Chandler shot back. Then she put up her dukes and came after Taylor who ran and hid behind Megan.

"Help me," Megan called, pleading to Abe who sighed and caught Chandler by the elbow then easily twisted her arm behind her back. Once again those years of karate lessons as a teenager came in handy.

"Cut it out," Abe said, holding Chandler's arm firmly until she stopped squirming.

"Okay! Okay! Uncle!"

"That's better."

"Taylor, apologize."

"I'm sorry," Taylor said, her face one of sweet innocence.

"And?"

"It won't happen again."

"It better not!" Chandler said, waiting until Abe looked away so she could pinch her on the arm.

"Ouch! Cut it out!"

Abe saw Susie seated at the table watching her with a sideways gaze. "Hi," she said when she realized Abe had seen her. "You look terrific."

"Thanks, you too." It was a hard statement to say, but it was true, so Abe said it. Susie was in yet another beautiful outfit. This time a strapless white eyelet dress with a fitted waist and a full skirt.

"Sit by me, Abe," Susie said. Abe was glad for the temporary reprieve from being called "Abigail," but Susie's sweet, friendly manner was unexpected . . . and disturbing. Abe couldn't help but wonder what Susie was up to now.

"Okay," she said and sat down. The server handed her a beer mug and offered up a foaming pitcher but Abe waved him away. "I'm driving," she said. "But I'd love a sweet tea."

Susie smiled. "I'm the designated driver too," she said. "That's funny. We always seem to have so much in common. We have many of the same friends. We wore the same dress the other night to the barbecue so we must have the same taste in fashion."

And the same taste in men, Abe thought but said nothing.

"Isn't that funny?" Susie asked, and Abe suspected that Susie may have been thinking the same thing she was.

"Yes."

"We should hang out together more. I know we'd be good friends."

Abe wanted to protest, but instead nodded. She'd go along with Susie, for now, although the thought of "hanging out" with her didn't appeal to Abe in the least.

"I want to ask you something," Susie said. The crowd at the table was noisy, and Abe was pleased to see that no one was paying much attention to them.

"Sure," Abe said. "Shoot."

"Is there anything going on between you and Wes?" Susie said it as lightly as she could, but Abe could tell that it was a question of enormous importance.

"Wes?"

"Yes."

"No," Abe said. She couldn't keep the grimace from her face. "We dated for a while, but that ended over six months ago."

"I know it ended six months ago," Susie said, looking intently into Abe's face. "But do you still . . . carry a torch for him?"

"What do you mean?"

"Do you still have a thing for him?"

"No," Abe said.

"Really?"

"Yes! I admit, I was a little bothered by the way things ended. But . . . I realize that Wes isn't my type." Susie looked relieved for a fleeting second, and Abe felt confused. "Why do you ask?"

This was a question Susie knew Abe would ask but hoped that she wouldn't. Her face paled a bit and she squirmed in her chair. "Well . . . umm . . . er . . . I was just curious. I've seen the way he flirts with you."

"That's just the way Wes is," Abe said. "He's a flirt."

The two young women eyed each other cautiously, and Abe had the sense that Susie wanted to say more but didn't. "What about you? Do you carry a torch for Wes?" Abe finally asked.

Susie stopped squirming nervously in her chair and then looked into Abe's face. "Yes," she said. There was almost a pleading quality in her voice. "And no. I mean, sometimes. I don't know. I like him, but he's so . . . so . . ."

"Fickle?"

"Yes. I guess that pretty much describes him. One minute he acts like I'm his favorite and the next minute, he's flirting with every woman in the room. Wes is fickle."

Abe watched her guardedly. "Yes he is, Susie, but so are you."

Susie said nothing for a moment, contemplating this bit of information. "I'm not as bad as Wes though," she said defensively. "Abe, can you do me a favor?"

"What's that?"

"Don't tell anyone what I told you . . . about Wes."

"I'm confused," Abe said, annoyance growing inside her. "I think Wes got the message about your feelings for him loud and clear at the shower."

"Really?" her face was worried. "Do you think he knows I like him?"

"No," Abe said, trying to keep her voice even. "I think he thinks that you like Jack."

"Do you think he's mad?" Susie asked.

"Probably." Abe wanted to tell her that she herself was fairly mad, but she didn't.

"Good," Susie said, surprising Abe again. "I hope he's furious with me."

"Why do you want Wes to be mad at you, Susie?"

"I don't want him to be mad at me," she said. "I just don't want him to think that I'm mooning over him either. Wes acts like I should follow him around like a little puppy dog. I guess I'm supposed to pretend not to notice when he's flirting with every girl in the room. He's so conceited. Not that he doesn't have good reason to be. I mean, look at him, he's gorgeous."

Abe blinked at Susie and tried to envision Wes in her mind's eye. She'd only recently stopped thinking of him as gorgeous herself, although now it felt like it'd been years.

"But he knows it!" Susie was saying, almost angrily. That's when she noticed that Abe was looking at her with a troubled expression on her face. "It's like this," she added. "Wes isn't like the other guys I've dated. With him, I don't know where I stand. He's so . . . I don't know. It's like one minute he likes me and the next, he's looking around to see who else is in the room. I can't pretend to understand him. All I know is that I don't like the feelings I have when he closes me off."

Abe was even more confused than ever. "Susie, what are you talking about?"

Susie's bottom lip was sticking out in a way that could only be described as a pout. "Wes," she said, exasperated. "Who do you think I'm talking about?"

"But what about Jack?" Abe asked, equally frustrated. "Jack?"

"Yes, Jack. You left the shower with him for a sunset drive, remember?" The "sunset drive" part came out far more biting than Abe planned but once said, she was pleased with her sarcasm.

"Oh, that," Susie said. "So, Jack gave me a ride home. So what? It wasn't as if Wes and I were together. Why can't I go with Jack? He's a great guy, Abe. I like him a lot."

They were both silent for a moment, considering each other. Abe had the sudden thought of telling Susie to back away from Jack, especially if she was interested in Wes. But, of course, she would never do such a thing. The idea of fighting over a man, any man, was appalling to Abe. It was so . . . so . . . barbaric.

Susie considered Abe thoughtfully, and then there was a look on her face, as if a light bulb suddenly went off right above her head. "Abe," she asked, her pretty hazel eyes growing larger. "Do you like Jack?"

Abe fought the urge to shake her. Couldn't she see that? Of course she liked Jack! And maybe Jack might like her too, if Susie wasn't in the picture. Abe hated herself for thinking such jealous thoughts and, in the end, she said nothing because Megan chose just that moment to appear. "Hey," she shouted. "This is my party! Why isn't everyone fawning over me? I'm the bride!"

"Sorry," Susie giggled and then launched into a discussion about the bridesmaid dresses and looking for a matching handbag.

Abe was left feeling puzzled and unsatisfied.

The rest of the evening was fun, but Abe never did find a chance to finish her conversation with Susie and she went to bed that night even more confused than ever.

Chapter Nine

"I can't believe I'm getting married tomorrow," Megan said, her voice breathless. Her face was a soft shade of pink and her eyes were moist and dewy. "It's going to rain tonight but the weatherman said it'll pass through quickly and be beautiful tomorrow. Just like I ordered."

"It's going to be perfect," Abe gushed. She'd arrived at the church early, as per Mrs. Randal's request. She was, after all, the maid of honor and, as such, it was her job to help with the many tasks involved with the wedding. The many, many, many tasks. Abe mentally ran down her to do list as she carried in an armload of shopping bags. It was gifts for the attendants and a shopping bag full of necessities that would be needed the next day while the wedding party got dressed: extra pantyhose, snack foods, first aid kit, nail polish remover, etc. Abe sighed. One more day and it would all be over.

The wedding coordinator called earlier and said she was running late—much to Mrs. Randal's annoyance. To help smooth over any bad feelings, Abe jumped in and greeted the members of the wedding party as they arrived and told them where to stand. She'd already memorized the drill and knew exactly what was expected of each and every member of the wedding party. Chandler arrived with Taylor and George. Chandler's boyfriend, Sean, had an emergency at work and would be meeting them later at the restaurant. Billy's parents and his brother Nathan arrived next. Then Erin and her husband, Derek, along with Megan's aunt and uncle and her cousin Alex. Next, Kasey arrived with Andrew.

Abe was nervous and flustered. She hated the anticipation and wished that everyone would get there so she could get the evening over with. She didn't want it to be that way, but her heart was pounding a mile a minute because she knew she would soon see Jack again and didn't know if she could manage to keep smiling. Every time someone appeared from the doorway, Abe felt her heart flip. Where was Susie? Where was Wes? But even more of a mystery, where was Jack? It was now five days since she'd last seen him. Five days of feeling like she was living in the bottom of a well.

Someone else was coming. Abe's heart skipped a beat as she heard the footsteps approach, but it was just the wedding coordinator.

"Finally," Mrs. Randal scolded, glaring at her.

"I apologize," the woman said, keeping her voice

steady and strong. "My ten-year-old isn't well and I needed to wait for my husband to get home from work before I could get here."

"I'm sorry about your daughter," Mrs. Randal snapped. "But that just isn't acceptable. Megan needs you here to . . ." But before she could finish her tirade, Megan interrupted her.

"Don't worry about it, Debra," Megan said, casting a dark look in her mother's direction. "It's perfectly understandable. As a matter of fact, I'm sure we can handle things here. Go home and take care of your little girl. We'll see you tomorrow."

The wedding coordinator blinked at Megan a few times, looking as if she wanted nothing more than to do just that. But instead she smiled and said, "Nonsense, Megan. My husband has everything under control at home. Right now we're going to go through what everyone needs to know for tomorrow, step by step until we get it right, okay?"

"Okay," Megan said. "But how about we run through it once? Then I insist you go home to your family. Everything will be perfect tomorrow. I'm not worried in the least bit." Debra nodded in agreement.

"Well, as long as everything goes smoothly . . ."

"So then, we have a deal?"

"It's a deal," Debra said, glancing cautiously at Mrs. Randal.

"Don't mind her," Megan whispered. "She's just nervous about tomorrow. I know we're going to be just fine. It's going to be a princess wedding."

Abe heard voices in the hallway. Someone was coming and they weren't alone. She kept her back to the door in hopes of not appearing too anxious, but she could tell by the exasperated expression on Megan's ' face just who it was behind her.

"Sorry we're late," Susie said breathlessly.

Abe turned and saw her as she walked through the doorway. Flushed and pretty, wearing a sophisticated black dress, with Wes at her side. Abe smiled and greeted them. She was comforted that Jack wasn't with Susie, but where was he?

Another ten minutes passed before he arrived. Abe's eyes went right to his. She didn't want to look at him so intently, but she just couldn't help it. She wanted to see his eyes. She knew that they would tell her what she wanted to know. Jack was looking at her too and their eyes locked, involuntarily, but only for a split second. There was something in his eyes that Abe couldn't identify. An expression that was a mixture of wounded pride and stubbornness but there was something else too. Jack had a look (was it her imagination?) of longing on his face.

"Hi," Wes said, smiling. Abe noted that he didn't look any the worse for wear. He was still irksomely handsome but he didn't have his usual brashness. She also noticed that despite the smile, Wes wore the unmistakable look of a man who'd recently suffered a blow to his ego. He was more subdued, more polite. His usual wandering eye stayed focused only on Susie. She, of course, was radiant and basking in the attention. She had one hand held tightly onto Wes's hand while the other hand reached out and touched Jack's elbow.

Megan looked at Susie with an annoyed expression on her face. "Susan," she said sharply. "Do you mind if I have a word with you in private?"

Susie looked surprised but wore a look of innocence. "I'm not that late, Megan," she said. "Please don't be mad at us."

"I'm not mad about tardiness," Megan said, her voice rising. "And I don't care about the time. I just need a minute with you . . . PRIVATELY."

Susie nodded and obediently followed Megan out into the hallway, smiling sweetly but looking startled. Kasey looked at Abe and smiled, a smug "I knew it would come to this" sort of look in her eyes. "Finally," she whispered to Abe who looked around her carefully to make certain they weren't overheard.

"I know," Chandler echoed from behind Kasey. "It's about time Megan told Susie off."

"What do you mean?" Abe whispered back.

"Ugh," Kasey groaned. "Susie's such a . . ."

"Kasey, don't," Chandler warned. "Susie's not always like this. I like her most of the time. It's just that being around all these men has made her crazy. And stupid."

"Definitely," Kasey said disgusted. "Crazy stupid, that's what she is. But to use Megan's wedding to make Wes jealous . . ."

"What are you talking about?" Abe asked.

"Come on, Abe," Kasey said. "Where have you been? Everyone knows Susie has it bad for Wes."

"And Jack," Abe said, the words sticking in her throat. "She likes them both. She just can't make up her mind—or at least she couldn't make up mind until the wedding shower. Now, obviously, she's picked Jack." Abe tried not to sound bitter but, even to her own ears, the last sentence sounded whiny.

"Where'd you get that idea?" Chandler said. "Susie's not interested in Jack, Abe, and she didn't have to make up her mind. She only flirts with Jack because she knows it drives Wes crazy."

"But she left the shower with Jack, remember?"

"Huh?" Kasey said baffled. "He just gave her a ride, Abe. You know, you really need to cut back on your maid-of-honor duties."

"Let me get you up to speed," Chandler said with a sigh. "This drama has been unfolding for weeks now, Abe. It's like this: Susie meets Wes. Susie likes Wes. Wes likes Susie until other women show up, then he starts to behave like . . . well, like Wes and flirts with all his former girlfriends. Ehem!"

"I never flirted with Wes," Abe protested. "I don't like him that way."

"You know that," Chandler said. "And I know that. But Wes doesn't know that. And Susie doesn't know that."

"Yeah," Kasey added. "To tell you the truth, I loved it when Susie started to give Wes a little taste of his own medicine. Except that she took it too far."

"Jack dance with me," Chandler mimicked in a high, silly voice. "We're going on a sunset drive. Barf!"

"I know," Kasey agreed. "But she sure got his attention, didn't she?'

"Yep," Chandler said. "I have to give credit where credit is due, although Susie's methods of pursuit are primitive. You have to admit, they've been quite effective, at least as far as Wes is concerned. He hasn't taken his eyes off her for a second, and I think he may even have cut back on his flirting."

"Yeah," Kasey said. "You may be right. But I'm not surprised. Everyone knows Wes only likes women who want nothing to do with him. Just like when you dated him, Abe. He was Mr. Wonderful for a while, wasn't he?"

"Yes," Abe admitted. "But then he dropped me like a hot potato." She said it in a matter-of-fact tone because for the first time it didn't hurt to say it. This time there was no sting of regret. This time she felt relieved.

"Yeah and he still flirts with you every chance he gets," Kasey added. "What a playboy! What woman in her right mind would be attracted to a man with those kinds of issues?"

"Susie," Chandler said rolling her eyes.

"But what about Jack?" Abe asked. "Where does he fall into this picture? I thought Susie liked him too. For Pete's sake, she left the shower with him!"

"That was nothing," Chandler said. "Susie asked Jack to give her a ride home so Wes would see her walking out with him. She knew it would drive him crazy. I know for a fact that Susie was home ten minutes later because she called me on my cell phone to ask me if Wes said anything about her leaving."

"What?" Abe gasped, but there was no time for a response because Susie came through the door with Megan following behind her. Megan looked pleased, and Susie looked flushed and unhappy.

"Now," Megan said in a strong, commanding voice.

"Let's get down to business. Debra needs to get home to her daughter."

The rest of the rehearsal went off without a hitch, with everyone doing exactly what they were supposed to do. Especially Susie, who wore an expression of eager helpfulness throughout the rest the rehearsal. Within an hour, they were headed to the restaurant.

The Madison was one of the best restaurants in Raleigh. It was known for delicious food and a pleasing décor. Megan couldn't have selected a better place for the rehearsal dinner. She'd even won the battle with her mother over the use of placecards at the table in hopes of creating a more casual atmosphere, but now she was the one barking out orders on who was to sit where.

"No, Wes," she said firmly. "I want you to sit right there, between Taylor and Susan. That's right. Chandler, you sit with Nathan. Perfect." Mrs. Randal watched the exchange with a sharp-eyed interest but said nothing. "Jack, would you mind taking a seat at the end. Then Abigail. Then Andrew. Then Erin and Derek. I want everyone to sit next to the person they will be walking down the aisle with tomorrow, boy-girl-boy-girl. That's it. Perfect."

Megan's madness was suddenly making sense now that she was finally in charge. Abe found herself next to Jack with Susie sitting next to Wes at the opposite end of the table. It was a seating arrangement that thrilled her, but frightened her too. She glanced at Jack, smiled coolly and avoided looking into his eyes as best she could. "Hello," she said in a voice that she hoped sounded sufficiently like a proper maid of honor. "How are you?"

"Good," he said. He was avoiding looking at her too, something that made Abe feel a sudden flash of anger. Why was he acting like she had the plague when he was the one who left the shower with Susie, she thought to herself. Then she remembered what Chandler said about Jack giving Susie a ride home—he did it because she asked him to. That bit of information brought a smile to Abe's face. She couldn't help it. Knowing that Susie was home ten minutes later made everything suddenly seem right. So Abe smiled at him and then he smiled back. He tried not to smile, but he couldn't help it. For a second, he smiled that heart-melting smile that Abe found so irresistible. There was something about him, a warmth and friendliness that made him smile even when he didn't want to. That smile made Abe forget he'd left the shower with Susie. Then she reminded herself that Susie asked him for a ride.

"What's up with Megan?" he asked.

"What do you mean?"

"The sudden seating arrangement," he said.

"She wants us to sit with the person we'll be walking down the aisle with tomorrow."

"Oh."

"Yep."

"Yep." Jack said nothing for a moment, and then he took a slow sip from his water glass. His manner was careful and composed. "I'm surprised she didn't change things around."

"What do you mean change things around?"

"I don't know. It's just that I think the maid of honor would have been given the first choice of where to sit at the rehearsal dinner at least. Although I guess you don't have to sit here for long."

Abe looked at him and tilted her head. "What do you mean?" she asked. "Don't let me stop you if you want to sit somewhere else."

"I'm just doing what I'm told to do," he said, his eyes meeting hers again. She met his gaze with one she hoped was icy cold.

"Me too."

"I'd have thought you would have asked Megan to pair you up with Wes," he said and Abe noticed his jaw tighten.

"Wes?" Abe said, wrinkling her nose. "Why would I want to be paired up with Wes?"

He looked at her, his eyes studying her face for a long moment. "Because . . ." he said slowly, his voice low. "Because I hear that you'd prefer it that way."

"Huh?"

Jack squinted at her and then looked even more baffled. "I hear that Wes and you used to date."

Abe nodded reluctantly. "Yes," she said. "It's true but we broke up a long time ago."

He nodded. "I heard," he said. "But spare me the details."

He said nothing for a moment than he gave her a long, steady look. There was a touch of frost in his usually warm voice.

"Is there something bothering you?" Abe finally said.

"Yeah," he said. "There is something bothering me."

"Well, perhaps you'd like to enlighten me!" she said abruptly.

"Perhaps I will," he snapped. "From what I hear, you'd like to see that old flame you had for Wes rekindled." His voice was low and the words came out in short bites, as if he couldn't stand to say them.

Abe tilted her head and looked at him as if he was crazy. "What old flame?" she said. "Who told you this nonsense?"

"Susan!"

"Susan?"

"Yes," he said, his voice suddenly not as tense as it was moments before. "She told me at the barbecue. Remember when she pulled me aside to talk? When we were . . . sitting on the bench?" His eyes were searching hers now. "She told me about how you and Wes had dated before. I think her exact words were that you were still crazy about him."

"What?" Abe couldn't believe her ears. She glanced over at Susie and saw that she was in a deep conversation with Wes, who seemed to be hanging onto her every word.

"I was surprised too," Jack said. "Somehow I can't picture you with a guy like Wes. He's always considered himself God's gift to women, and I thought you'd see through all that but Susan was very clear."

"Clear about what?"

"She said that you wanted to work things out with Wes and that you were hoping the wedding would be a fresh start for the two of you. She asked me . . . not to interfere." His voice dropped to a whisper as he repeated the conversation.

"Susie asked you to not interfere with me . . . and Wes?"

"Yes."

"But it's not true," Abe said, her voice strained. "I never said I wanted to rekindle ANYTHING with ANYONE."

Jack was silent for a moment, studying her face. "It sounded odd to me," he finally said. "Because I'd gotten the feeling that you and I were beginning to get to know each other. I even thought . . . never mind what I thought. Susan said you were crazy about Wes and she asked me not to come between you and him. I just figured, who was I to stand in your way? So I agreed with her."

"You left with her!"

"I didn't leave with her," he protested. "I gave her a ride home. She asked me to."

"Oh," Abe said. The information Jack told her sunk in slowly. She cocked her head sideways and looked as if she was in deep thought. "I'm not crazy about Wes," she said at last. "I mean, it's true we dated but that was a long time ago—it's been at least six months since we broke up. It wasn't exactly an epic romance to begin with. He dropped me."

"He's an idiot."

"I know, he can be. But I didn't see it at first. Wes and I are friends now, Jack. We get along well enough but I don't have a crush on him, if that's what you think. I don't know why Susan would tell you such a thing."

Susie happened to look their way just then and saw

that Abe and Jack were sitting together and talking with their heads so close, they were almost touching. She also noticed the way they were both shooting quick, bewildered glances in her direction. She took in their body language and the expressions on their faces and knew immediately that she was in deep, deep trouble. She smiled at them warily and waved.

"I think I know what's going on," Abe whispered, still watching Susie. "Jack, Susie . . . Susan is the one who likes Wes."

"I've gathered that much," Jack said. "But that's not exactly a mystery. Despite what she says, it's obvious that Susan is the one who's crazy about Wes. I've seen the way she looks at him and the way she flirts with me whenever he's around. I'm not stupid. But I believed her when she asked me to keep my distance from you. I thought she was taking some high road for you because she's your friend. I assumed that she spoke to me because she wanted both of us not to mess up your chances with Wes." He spat out the last sentence as if it was something that tasted bad.

"I don't have a thing for Wes!" she said and quickly realized she was speaking loud enough for others to hear because Kasey looked at her with raised eyebrows. "I mean, I . . . I like Wes, but not in that way," she said, softer. "Wes likes women who are more . . . aloof. He likes women who play hard to get. Do you know the type?"

"Yes. Painfully. And I can't stand it when women play stupid games like that. Isn't it better to be honest with someone? Even if they don't feel the same way, it's better than . . ." He stopped mid-sentence and looked at her. "Isn't it better to just put your cards on the table?"

"Yes."

"To be honest with you, I was wondering why you didn't do just that with Wes. I didn't think you were the game-playing type."

"I'm not. At least, I don't think I am."

"You're not, not from what I've seen of you. But then again, I haven't known you for long. Or at least I told myself I didn't know you. You don't seem like the type, but I just met you. I guess I should have trusted my instincts more and not listened to Susan. Now I think I understand things. She's the one who's crazy about Wes." He looked at Susie with an expression of dumbfounded surprise and shook his head. "I've been an idiot."

"Me too."

"Look, Abigail," he said, turning to her. "I don't know what to say to you. I thought *you* were the one who was sending out mixed signals. It bothered me because since the first time I laid eyes on you, I've wanted to get to know you better. And the more I saw of you, the more I liked you." Abe felt herself melting again. "And as long as I'm putting my cards on the table— finally—I might as well tell you that I haven't been able to get my mind off you since the day I met you. But this situation with Wes is driving me crazy. Susan said . . . I didn't want to stand in your way if Wes was what you wanted."

"But, Jack," Abe said. "It isn't true."

"Good. I can't tell you how glad it makes me feel to hear that."

"Good? How is this good? I thought Susie was my friend."

"It's the best news I've heard all month. And don't take it personally. She would have told anyone anything if she thought it would help her get Wes's attention. I should have a chat with him and let him know what's going on."

"No," Abe said. "Don't do that. It's Megan and Billy's wedding day tomorrow. Just let it go. Besides, you can't say that Susie doesn't know what she wants. She should have a go with Wes. She's earned it."

"That's true," he said. "And they do kind of look good together."

"They do. In a way, they're the perfect couple."

"Maybe," he said. "But for how long? He'll run away once she stops playing games and lets him know how she really feels."

"He might, but I don't think he will this time. Wes was due to get a taste of his own medicine. Maybe it will be a good lesson for him. Besides I think he likes her. Really likes her. And who knows? Maybe she'll be the one who will make Wes finally grow up."

Abe didn't feel angry anymore. She just felt drained. The past few weeks had been more of a strain on her than she realized. She allowed herself a deep breath and felt suddenly much more at ease. She looked at Jack and saw that he was looking at her. His eyes were soft and questioning.

"Well," he said. "This is certainly an interesting new development, isn't it?"

"Yes. It certainly is."

"So. Does this mean you're eligible after all?"

"It depends. Eligible for what?"

"Eligible for me."

Abe smiled. "Yeah," she said. "I'm eligible."

Dinner arrived and the evening wore on, except Abe and Jack were no longer aware of the party around them. Now they only had eyes for each other. They ate and talked and quickly forgot about the other people at the table. Even Megan was left off of their cloud.

After dinner Abe chose her moment to approach Susie carefully. She waited until Wes stepped away before she made her move. Never one to beat around the bush, she asked her a question without a trace of anger in her voice, "Susie, why did you tell Jack that I was trying to get back with Wes?"

"Um . . . I . . ." Susie stammered. "Aren't you? Gee, I thought you were. Do you mean to say you're not attracted to Wes? I thought you liked him, Abe. Oops. Sorry about that."

"Oops?"

"I'm sorry, Abe. I didn't mean anything by it. Really, I didn't. Jack and I were just making small talk. I happened to mention that you and Wes once dated and I . . . It was a completely innocent mistake." Susie smiled nervously, talking too quickly, like a child who'd been caught sneaking cookies from a jar.

"You pulled him aside at the shower and specifically told him that I was interested in Wes. Why'd you say that when you know it isn't true?"

Her face crumbled. "I'm sorry, Abe. Really I am. I

didn't know that it wasn't true. Not really. It always seemed as if you still had a thing for Wes." Genuine tears sprang to Susie's eyes and Abe felt a stab of remorse. The last thing she ever wanted to do was make someone cry. Even Susie. Other people crying made Abe want to cry, so tears sprung to her eyes too.

"Don't do that," Abe said. "Not when I'm trying to chew you out. Susie, I think you told Jack a lie so that it would make Wes jealous."

"No," she said quickly. "That wasn't it at all. I saw that Jack was interested in you, Abe. I thought if I fanned the flame, you know, maybe made him a little jealous of Wes . . . I thought I was helping you. Listen, Megan already chewed me out once tonight. Please don't you do it too."

Abe watched her carefully; the tears were threatening to fall any second but Abe was determined to say what she wanted to say. "Susie, it's wrong to use people. It's wrong to play with their emotions. It's wrong and it's childish and it's mean. Other people have feelings too."

And with that, Susie's tears started to flow. "I'm sorry, Abe," she said, her pretty voice breaking. "That's not what I meant to do. I'm so sorry I upset anyone. I . . ." But she never finished her sentence because she suddenly darted into the direction of the restroom, trying to hide the tears that were now spilling down her cheeks as she fled.

Abe watched her journey with deep sadness and pity all the while fighting back her own tears. She was immediately sorry she'd chosen that moment to confront

Susie. She wished she'd waited until they could have talked more privately.

"That didn't go well," Abe told Jack glumly when she returned to her seat. "I feel worse than ever."

"Don't feel too bad for Susan," he said. "I have the feeling she's going to find someone to comfort her." He nodded in the direction of Wes who'd seen Susie's dramatic exit and was in hot pursuit with a determined look on his face.

"I made her cry," Abe said miserably, a tear spilling down her own cheek. "I don't like making people cry."

"She is pitiful, isn't she?" Jack said, taking Abe by the hand and squeezing it.

"Yes, and she can't help it if she's a big dope."

"No, she can't," he said. "And there was no real harm caused, right?"

"No," Abe said, and she felt Jack pull her closer.

"So?" he said. "Let's put it all behind us now."

"Okay."

"Okay, then. Where were we?"

Chapter Ten

Abe opened her eyes slowly. For a moment, she forgot what day it was and enjoyed the deliciousness of snuggling comfortably into her warm, cozy bed. Daylight was just beginning to peek through her bedroom window. It was too early to get out of bed, and she enjoyed the precious moments of drowsiness. She waited to drift back to sleep, letting her thoughts return to the sweet dreams she'd had the night before. She dreamed of Jack and the way he'd kissed her after the rehearsal dinner. She remembered the way his heart pounded so close to hers and how good it felt to be held tightly in his arms. So real was the memory, she barely noticed that there was something different about the world outside of her snug, comfy bed. Something that would cut short the slow, pleasant waking she sought.

Slowly but surely, it crept into Abe's mind that this day was more important than other days. Today was the big day (at long last), but that thought made Abe want to burrow deeper into the covers. A feeling of unease settled over her. She opened her eyes with a start, suddenly understanding the reason for her worry. It wasn't that it was still dark outside. No, that just meant there was still more time to sleep. Nor was it the pressing knowledge that today was going to be a very busy one. That didn't concern her in the least. It was something else. There was a soft noise, almost inaudible, that was coming from outside her bedroom window. A gentle murmur just outside her covers, a sound so subtle, she barely heard it at all. Abe sat up and listened carefully. Oh no, it couldn't be! This couldn't possibly happen! NOT TODAY!

But it was. The murmur she heard was suddenly as loud and clear as a ringing alarm clock and it was equally jarring. Outside of Abe's bedroom window it was raining.

Not just raining. It was pouring.

She disentangled herself from the cocoon of blankets and climbed out of bed. She walked to the window, folded back the curtains and with a sinking heart peered out to the street below, silently praying that her ears were playing a trick on her. But they weren't. It was indeed raining outside—and it was a hard, determined, miserable rain at that.

She stared glumly out the window trying to acknowledge what was happening. Why today of all days? Especially after the long chain of one beautiful day after another that they'd enjoyed, each one more perfect and gorgeous than the one before. Why did Megan's good luck so heartlessly run out? Abe scanned the dark sky. A glance at the clock on her nightstand told her that it wasn't still nighttime at all. It was dark because it was a gloomy, rainy day outside. She studied the clouds again, looking for some sign of sunshine through the clouds but there was none to be seen. The sky was gray and the rain was falling as if it would never stop.

Abe picked up the receiver on the pink princess telephone on her night table and dialed a familiar phone number. "Megan?" she said when she heard the strained and unhappy voice on the other end of the line.

"I know!" her best friend wailed. Abe could tell by her voice that the monumental disappointment of the weather had pushed the bride to the breaking point. Megan was in complete meltdown.

"I'll be right over," Abe said.

She hung up the phone and sprang into action. She quickly packed up the things she'd need for the day, mentally running down the list of items as she raced through the room. She'd wisely packed up her makeup, shoes, and other essentials the night before and the duffel bag was waiting for her by the door. Her maid-of-honor gown hung on the hook on the back of the door, covered in plastic. Abe pulled on a pair of old, faded blue jeans and a T-shirt and ran a brush through her hair. She brushed her teeth but skipped everything else. She'd get dressed at Megan's house. Maybe they could somehow salvage the plans if they moved forward as if nothing was wrong. Minutes later she was bounding down the steps and shouting a good-bye to her parents.

"I'm going to Megan's," she called. "I'll see you at the wedding."

"Tell her not to worry," Mrs. Gibson said. "Rain on a wedding day is good luck."

"I'll tell her, but I don't think she'll buy it."

Abe could tell that the rain had begun the night before, probably after the members of the wedding party had gone to sleep for the night. There were a few broken branches scattered on the street, a sure sign that a storm recently passed through. Abe knew exactly the sort of storm too—a storm that was hardly rare for a North Carolina June. The wind blew and the thunder rumbled while she'd slept, peacefully dreaming of sweet, soft kisses. Now all that was left was the rain. Buckets and buckets of rain were coming down as if it would never stop. Abe pushed the buttons on her car radio until she found a weather report that confirmed her worst fears. The weatherman said the rain would likely last until that evening—or possibly the late afternoon. But looking at the sky behind her windshield, she feared the worst. She'd lived in North Carolina all her life and knew that sky well. It was going to rain all day long.

When Abe arrived at Megan's house, she found her sitting at the kitchen table with Erin. They both were glumly looking out the big bay window watching the rain with sad, brown eyes. Occasionally, they would glance at each other with worried, anxious expressions on their faces. Frequently one sister would offer a word of either encouragement or doom, depending on their particular level of panic at that given moment. Megan was wearing her favorite raspberry pink silk pajamas and her old fluffy bedroom slippers, while Erin was huddled in a plaid flannel bathrobe. Derek wisely stayed in bed, far away from the Randal women who are not known for keeping their heads in a crisis. Every moment or so, one sister would warily dare a peek at their mother. But there was nothing that either could say or do that could counterbalance the storm that was brewing there.

Mrs. Randal was pacing the floor and muttering to herself. Her face was pinched and pink and her eyes were angry and darting. Every few moments, she would huff to the bay window and look outside. Each time she would see that it was indeed raining and she would become even more agitated. "I can't believe this is happening," she said and returned to her pacing, which was actually more of a stomp than anything else. "What are we going to do? What are we going to DO? This is so unfair!"

"Everything's going to be all right, Mrs. R.," Abe said, sizing up the potentially volatile situation.

"It isn't going to be all right!" Mrs. Randal screeched, angry tears welling up in her eyes. "Everything's ruined!"

Abe and Erin gave each other anxious looks and grimaced. Here it comes, their knowing eyes seemed to say. Abe reminded herself of all the planning that poor Mrs. Randal had done over the past year. But months and months of careful and meticulous preparation couldn't stop it from raining today. Not even for Megan. And to Mrs. Randal, rain was the cruelest blow of all.

Of course, the mother of the bride falling apart was not helping the situation much either.

"It's going to be all right," Abe said, this time with a firmness in her voice that surprised even her. Even to her own ears, her voice sounded calm but strong, almost angry. Abe knew that reacting to a hissy fit with another hissy fit was risky, and she was determined to stay calm, no matter how crazy Mrs. Randal became. But somebody needed to do something. This was Megan's wedding day!

Abe's voice must have had the right amount of conviction to it because as soon as the sentence was spoken, Erin stood up from the table. "Abe's right," she said. "Mom, you need to chill out! Everything isn't ruined. We've all worked too hard for too long for things to fall apart now. This isn't the end of the world. Megan's going to have a great wedding today, Mom. You'll see."

Megan looked from her sister to Abe and then, finally, to her mother. Her face was pale, but she was now sticking out her chin in that stubborn way of hers. That's when Abe knew everything was going to be all right.

"Of course I'm going to have a wonderful wedding," Megan said, as if any other alternative was too preposterous to consider. "Everything is going to be perfect. And, Mom, Erin's right, you're not helping. Get a grip on yourself!"

"But the rain—"

"A little rain won't kill us," Megan said, her brown eyes flashing angrily. "You're not made of sugar, you know! I won't melt and neither will you. I'll still be a beautiful bride, and I'm still going to get married today. Rain or no rain, I'm having a perfect wedding! Now get your butt moving! We have a wedding to put on."

With that, Megan tossed back her long, glossy hair and headed out of the kitchen. Abe and Erin followed behind her like baby ducklings following their mama. "Have another cup of coffee, Mom," Erin called, over her shoulder. "Pull yourself together and then come up and help us get ready. And you better be smiling the next time I see you!"

Mrs. Randal looked at the three young women glaring at her, a dour expression on her face. "I'll be fine in ten minutes," she finally said, sticking her chin out too. "I want to be mad for a few more minutes before I spring into my mother-of-the-bride mode. Megan's right. We aren't made of sugar, and we won't melt. Besides, rain on a wedding day is good luck, right?"

"Right," Erin said and flashed a smile. "Now hop to it. I better get in the bathroom first before Derek starts hogging it!"

And, with that, they disappeared up the steps.

"Good job," Abe said, once they were in Megan's bedroom.

"Thanks for your help. My mom woke up at the crack of dawn and she's been having a panic attack ever since. I was thinking about slapping her when you got here."

"She'll be okay. Your mom has a black belt in event planning, remember? She can handle a little rain."

"Of course she can. She just needed to fall apart a little. She'll be all right in a few minutes. To tell you the truth, I'm glad that she isn't hovering over me for a change. It will give me and you some time to catch up. I feel like I haven't spoken to you in days, although we've seen each other constantly. This has been such a whirl, hasn't it, Abe? I don't want it all to go by without us getting a chance to share it. Let's take a few minutes and catch our breath."

"Let's." Abe sat on the edge of Megan's bed and watched her friend return to her usual, bouncy, sassy self.

"So," Megan said. "What's new with you?"

"Other than your wedding? Not much."

"Let me rephrase my question then. What the heck is going on with you and Susie . . . and Wes . . . and Jack?"

"What have you heard?"

"Just that she ran into the bathroom in tears last night because you blasted her about something. Kasey told me that you and Susie were in an argument. What's up with that?"

"We did have an argument," Abe confessed. "I'm sorry it happened at your rehearsal dinner though. I feel terrible about it now. In hindsight, I wish I'd waited to confront her."

"Confront her about what?"

"It's a long story. Let's just say that Susie and I needed to clear the air."

"Come on, Abe," Megan groaned. "Tell me what happened!"

Abe hesitated. "You've got enough on your mind today, Megan. I'll tell you all about it when you and Billy get back from your honeymoon."

"No way! This is good dirt. Besides, I'm trying to

keep my mind occupied on other matters right now. If I think too much about the wedding and the weather, I'm going to pop! Tell me what happened last night!"

"Okay, okay. I'll tell you." Abe leaned in closer and spoke in a soft, calm voice. "Remember how Susie said she wanted dibs on the groomsmen?"

"Yes. That's just so Susie. No one calls dibs on human beings! They call dibs on the front seat of the car or the last piece of fried chicken."

"Well, Susie called dibs on the men in your wedding party and, apparently, she was very serious when she said it."

"So I see."

Abe looked at Megan's excited face and felt immediately guilty. "You don't need to hear about this now. You have too much happening, what with you getting married today and all. Let's talk about something else."

"Abe!" Megan shouted. "What happened last night?"

"All right. All right! This sounds so silly now, but . . . all right, here goes nothing: Susie apparently has a thing for Wes."

"No kidding. I hadn't noticed."

"I guess I was the only one who didn't see that one. I thought she saw your wedding as some kind of guy buffet. Anyway, in the case of Wes Vaughn, Susie decided to forego the more conventional rules of attraction. With Wes she wanted to take the bull by the horn, so to speak. Apparently, she'd heard about his reputation as a ladies' man so Susie decided she'd beat him at his own game."

"I'd noticed that she'd taken the fine art of flirting to

a whole new level," Megan said. "I'm not blind, Abe. I've seen how much Susie flirts and giggles and flounces around the other guys when Wes is around. To tell you the truth, I've enjoyed watching it. Wes's response has been poetic justice. I think it's killing him—and I mean that in an amusing way."

"I think you're right. But Susie's especially been flirting with—"

"Jack. I know. Susie's been flirting with Jack to make Wes jealous. I know all about that. That's why I pulled her out into the hallway last night. I told her to knock it off because she was making everyone sick."

"I was wondering what that was all about," Abe said.

"Someone had to do it."

"Thanks," Abe said. "But you don't know the whole story. There's more to it than Susie flirting with Jack to make Wes jealous. Something happened that I don't think you know about."

"What's that?"

"Susie told Jack that I was interested in Wes and asked him to steer clear of me."

Megan's eyes popped open. "Say what?"

"She told him that I wanted to rekindle my burning desires for Wes and asked him not to interfere with our epic romance."

"No! Susie did WHAT? I'm going to have to knock that girl into next week!"

"Calm down, Meg. It's all under control now. Fortunately, Jack asked me about it. If he hadn't, I never would have known myself. Apparently Susie wanted Jack all to herself in hopes it would shake up Wes."

"And that's why you had an argument with Susie at the rehearsal dinner?"

"Yep."

"What did she say?"

"She said she thought she was doing me a favor. She said she thought I did have a thing for Wes. And she said that she was trying to fan Jack's flame for me by making him jealous of Wes. She said she thought she was helping me. I told her that I thought she was trying to help herself. I accused her of wanting to make Wes jealous of Jack—a scheme that seems to be working, by the way."

Megan was watching Abe with an expression of horror. "Run this all by me again, toots. It's obvious we've got a lot more catching up to do."

Abe explained the story again, only slower this time, leaving out no detail including the kiss she'd shared with Jack at the bridal shower.

"I told you you'd like him!" Megan said, her face breaking into a huge grin. "I told you so! Why don't you ever listen to me?"

"Yeah, yeah," Abe said. "You were right about a guy—for once! Don't let it go to your head! And don't let it inspire you to further matchmaking."

"And why didn't you tell me you and Jack were smooching?" Megan demanded. "That's some rather juicy information to forget to tell your best friend about, isn't it?"

"I was too embarrassed," Abe admitted. "All I knew was that one minute Jack was kissing me and the next he was leaving the bridal shower with Susie. It was mortifying! Little did I know, that was about the time Susie told him that I had the hots for Wes, not for him. And she asked him for a ride home."

"I remember," Megan said, rolling her eyes. "It was that sunset drive, wasn't it?"

"Ugh!" Abe groaned. "See what I mean. It was all too silly to tell you, what with the shower and the barbecue and . . . well, you know the whole story now, Megan. My life has been on a roller coaster for the past month. We'll have to go on a long shopping trip after your honeymoon so we can hash it all over about a thousand times. But for now, I don't want you to worry about my love life for another second."

"But, Abe, I like worrying about your love life. And I like Jack. I want him to be your boyfriend. Is that too much for a bride to ask of her maid of honor?"

"Megan! I didn't say he was my boyfriend. I said we kissed. A couple of times."

"Did you like it?"

"Yeah. I did."

"How much? A lot or a little?"

"Shut up," Abe groaned. "I said I liked it. That's all you need to know, nosy."

"That's a start. I think you and Jack are cute together. And I think he likes you too."

"You do?" Abe was blushing now. "How do you know that?"

"I don't know. Just a feeling. But I'm not the only one who thinks that way. Billy has noticed that Jack gets this goofy look on his face whenever you're around. He thinks Jack likes you too. Billy's going to bust a gut when he finds out that you and Jack are a hot topic. This is so cool!"

Abe felt her face flush deeper, and Megan squeezed her hand until it hurt. "Ouch!"

"Abe?" Megan asked. "Do you like him? I mean *really* like him?"

"Yes."

"How much?"

"A little."

"Just a little?"

"Maybe more than a little."

"How much more than a little?"

"A lot more than a little," Abe said, feeling almost giddy saying it. "And I don't know why. I mean, I guess I know why, but . . . I don't understand it. Every time I see Jack, I get all squishy inside. I've never felt this way before, Megan. Do you know what I mean?"

"Hello," Megan said, tossing her head back and laughing. "Bride here! I know exactly what you mean, Abe."

"I guess you might know what I mean, huh?"

Megan smiled a look of blissful happiness on her face. "Cool," she said.

Just then there was pounding at the door. "Megan!" Mrs. Randal shouted. "Haven't you gotten in the shower yet? The rest of the girls will be here soon!"

Chapter Eleven

The room was hot and stuffy and getting noisier by the moment.

"Somebody took my pantyhose!"

"Where's my lipstick?"

Eight young women in various stages of dress were crowded around Megan's standing mirror. They were showered and perfumed and their nails were all given a coat of shiny pink polish. They'd eaten every bite of food from the tray of muffins and pastries Mrs. Randal thoughtfully set out for them. Donna, the hairstylist, was finishing up with the last woman's updo and the rain was still beating a steady patter against the window pane. Abe stepped gingerly into her gown, careful not to move her head and upset the delicate balance of her hair.

"Zip me up, sweetpea," Abe said, turning her back to Kasey who obliged, careful not to damage her nails.

Mrs. Randal burst into the room. "Okay, ladies," she

shouted. "Everyone get downstairs! The photographer wants to get some pictures of the bride getting ready, and I have to set up the room. Y'all scoot! You included, Megan! I'll call you when I'm ready."

As predicted, Megan's mother had shaken off her morning breakdown and was now tearing through the house like a drill sergeant on a rampage, snapping orders at anyone who dared not move fast enough. The young women piled out of Megan's bedroom and headed down the steps. Abe was relieved to be out of the hot, crowded room, and she wondered if she should dare risk a sip of iced tea.

"Whew!" Susie said, looking at her with a tentative smile on her lips. "It was hot in there. Would you like to come with me to find something to drink? I'm dying of thirst."

Abe gave her a careful look, undecided if she was ready to forgive her or not. "Me too," she said, trying on a stiff smile for size. She was still shocked by Susie's dastardly deed, and she was over feeling guilty for confronting her. But Abe also knew that it was Megan's wedding day and was willing to postpone her troubles for a few days. Susie was pleased that Abe was speaking to her. They'd spent the afternoon carefully avoiding each other while they'd dressed, polite but careful to leave as much space as possible between them.

"You look gorgeous," Susie said, her voice low. "And I'm not just saying that because you're mad at me. I mean it, Abe. You're beautiful."

"Thanks. You are too. And I'm not just saying it because you said it to me."

The women eyed each other guardedly, testing the air around them for signs of conflict.

"I'm sorry, Abe," Susie said after an awkward silence. "I'm so ashamed of myself. Can you ever forgive me?"

"I don't know yet," Abe said. She knew that was not what Susie wanted to hear, but it was the way she felt inside. The honesty felt good.

Susie's face fell. "I understand," she said. "I deserve it. I don't blame you for being mad at me, Abe, and I hope you can forgive me someday."

"I'm going to try," Abe said and she meant that too.

"Fair enough," Susie said. "I'm going to try to be a better person." Susie carefully took Abe's hand in hers and squeezed it. Abe took the gesture as an offer of peace and squeezed her hand in return. "I don't know about you," Susie said, her voice cracking, "but I'm parched. Let's go see if we can scare up something to drink."

"Okay. Let's do that."

They filed out of Megan's bedroom along with the others. Meanwhile the rain continued to fall, and Mrs. Randal went to work clearing Megan's bedroom of the tornado of clothes, makeup and hair paraphernalia that was scattered around the room. She quickly restored the room to pristine condition by shoving anything unsightly into Megan's closet and slamming the door shut. She then ushered the photographer in to take pictures.

The photographer took pictures of Megan gazing into the carved wooden standing mirror that was purchased just for this occasion and he took pictures of the bridesmaids surrounding her. He took pictures of Megan and Erin and pictures of Megan and her mother. Then he took pictures of Megan and Abe, smiling cheek to cheek, and then more pictures of Mrs. Randal smiling down on the bride and more pictures of the bridesmaids. Picture after picture after picture after picture. It seemed like hours of taking pictures. Abe felt as if her face was frozen in a state of perpetual smile.

"Go away," Megan said with mock annoyance to the photographer as he swooped in for a close-up.

"Just a few more," he said, ignoring her completely.

"Hurry up, girls!" Mrs. Randal was shouting. "The limo will be here any minute!"

The women assembled themselves in the living room, giggling excitedly and talking amongst themselves . . . and not a moment too soon. A knock on the door announced the arrival of the limousine. Next thing they knew, they were sitting in the back of a long, white limo and headed for the church. The trip to the car was a slow one since each woman was required to hold her dress high as they were escorted along, one at a time by Mr. Randal and the limo driver who held umbrellas over their heads as they moved along. So intense was the effort to ensure that no hairdo or gown was damaged, no one noticed that the rain had slowed to a drizzle.

Chapter Twelve

Jack was standing in the doorway of the church when they pulled up to the curb. Abe saw him as soon as the limo pulled into the parking lot and felt her stomach drop.

"Where's Billy?" Megan called to him with panic in her voice. "He's not supposed to see me until the ceremony!"

"It's okay, Meg," Taylor told her. "I don't see him. He's not anywhere near here yet. Don't worry. We'll keep watch while you sneak in."

"No," Mrs. Randal said. "We'll let you girls out here and then Megan and I will go around to the back entrance. Abigail, you know where to go, right?"

"Right."

The limo driver put the car in park and came around with the umbrella and, once again, began the slow route of delivering the women to the door one at a time, except this time he was solo because Mr. Randal was banned from the limo due to gender segregation.

"What are you doing?" Jack asked Abe after she was led up the short staircase to the front door.

"What do you mean?"

"Why are you all under an umbrella? It's not raining."

Abe looked at him and blinked. She hadn't noticed it until then, but the rain had indeed stopped. There was even a faint hope in the air that the sun might even peek out from behind the clouds that day. "It stopped?" she asked, grinning from ear to ear.

"Yeah," he said. "It stopped. You didn't think it was going to rain for Megan and Billy's wedding, did you?"

"I should have known better than that!" Abe said and gave him a hard high five.

The limo driver shrugged and snapped the umbrella closed. "What do you know?" he said. "It's going to be a nice night after all."

The church was a large, old building with graceful southern charm and more than adequate to accommodate the two hundred expected guests. Abe stood on the sweeping porch and looked out over the parking lot just as the first happy ray of sunshine peeked through the clouds. She looked at Jack and smiled.

"You're beautiful," he said and kissed her.

"Thanks," she said. "You don't look so bad yourself." Then he took her hand in his and led her inside. She almost forgot it was her job to make sure everybody got to where they needed to be. Luckily Jack remembered and pointed her in the right direction. He then gave her one last kiss and said, "I'll see you at the ceremony. Good luck." Then he disappeared down the hallway.

"All right, ladies," Abe shouted, rounding up the women and trying to forget the delicious taste of Jack's kiss. "We're going to make this the prettiest, best, gosh darn, rooting-tooting wedding anyone's ever seen. Right?"

"Right," the women echoed, unconvincingly.

"I can't hear you!" Abe shouted.

"Right!" they shouted back.

She led them to the tight room next to the chapel where they waited for the wedding planner, who'd done an excellent job of getting everything ready at the church. Each of the church pews were decorated with beautiful sprays of lavender and bright pink flowers that smelled heavenly. Everything was ready. Abe felt suddenly nervous about her role for the day. She'd never been a maid of honor before and the responsibility suddenly weighed on her. Please, she prayed, let this be everything Megan wants it to be.

Finally, the organ music began to play and the women were told it was time to begin. Abe watched as Billy's mother was led to her seat by Nathan. Next, she saw Mrs. Randal being led down the aisle by Alex. He walked her to the front pew on the bride's side and kissed her on the cheek.

"Okay, ladies," Debra, the wedding planner, said. "Line up."

The bridesmaids were first, one at a time. Kasey, then Chandler, then Susie, then Taylor. Their dresses and hair were pristine, despite the earlier poor weather. It was probably one of the few times anyone saw Taylor not wearing her favorite color—orange—at least in some small way. Abe was certain she'd snuck it in somewhere and, sure enough, later learned that Taylor wore a bright orange garter. Next came Erin, smiling sweetly. All the women walked down the aisle slowly, as they'd been told to, smiling at everyone along the way. All too soon it was Abe's turn to go. She took her first steps bravely, looking out at the guests with a beaming smile on her face. The aisle seemed a lot longer than it was at the rehearsal. She kept her eye on the altar, also smiling and nodding as she made her way down the long, long aisle. Finally, she reached her destination. The bridesmaids and groomsmen were right where they were supposed to be, waiting for the bride at the altar. Everyone was smiling, but Abe didn't notice any of them because she was too busy noticing Jack. He was looking at her too, a big smile on his face. For a second, they were the only ones there. Her knees wobbled, and she forgot all about the event that was going on around her. But then Jack winked at her and she slowly returned to earth. Abe winked back.

Just then the organ music began to play the wedding march. The guests turned around to see Megan as she took her first step down the aisle. There was a lump in Abe's throat when she saw her. Megan's gown was so beautiful. Her hair was shinier than ever, even with the updo and headpiece. Megan's eyes met Abe's and, for a second, she froze. But then Abe smiled at her and Megan smiled back, a little frightened, but brave and sure. She began her slow walk down the aisle.

At first, she walked too quickly, almost dragging her poor father along behind her. But he planted his feet firmly to the floor and held tightly onto her elbow until she remembered that she was supposed to walk at a slower pace. She wore a strapless, body-hugging white silk gown that was exactly what she wanted, simple and elegant. In her arms, she carried a large bouquet of red roses that cascaded down the front of her dress. The train fell down her back, but stayed clear of her pretty face. Abe could see she was terrified, but her eyes were fixed on Billy, who was standing at the altar waiting for her with a surprisingly relaxed demeanor. She walked down the aisle, slower now, but still faster than her escort and still pulling him behind her. When she finally reached the altar, her father turned to Billy and shook his hand. He then gave Megan a big, sloppy kiss on her cheek and handed her over to Billy, who firmly took her by the hand and smiled.

"Dearly beloved," the minister began once the organ music subsided. "We are gathered together here in the sight of God—and in the face of this company—to join together this man and this woman in holy matrimony . . ."

Abe felt tears spring to her eyes and she saw that Jack was watching her from the other side of the altar, but his reassuring smile only made her feel even more sentimental. For a moment she didn't hear what the minister said because she was too busy smiling back at Jack.

"We are here today to witness the joining in marriage of William Mark Meegan and Gwendolyn Francine Megan Randal. This occasion marks the celebration of their love and commitment to each other as they begin their life together. Who gives this woman in marriage to this man?

"Her mother and I," said Mr. Randal with a booming but shaky voice.

"Do you William Mark Meegan take Gwendolyn Francine Megan Randal to be your wife—to live together in the holy state of matrimony? Will you love her, comfort her, honor and keep her, in sickness and in health, for richer, for poorer, for better, for worse, in sadness and in joy, to cherish and continually bestow upon her your heart's deepest devotion, forsaking all others, keep yourself only unto her as long as you both shall live?"

"I will," Billy said.

"Do you Gwendolyn Francine Megan Randal take William Mark Meegan to be your husband—to live together in the holy state of matrimony? Will you love him, comfort him, honor and keep him, in sickness and in health, for richer, for poorer, for better, for worse, in sadness and in joy, to cherish and continually bestow upon him your heart's deepest devotion, forsaking all others, keep yourself only unto him as long as you both shall live?"

"I will," said Megan. Abe saw the tears in her eyes but her voice remained clear and strong.

"What token of your love do you offer?" the minister asked and Jack quickly fished into his pocket and produced two gold rings. He handed them to him.

The minister took the rings and handed one to Billy. He smiled and slipped the ring on Megan's finger as he repeated the vows the minister gave him. Then Megan did the same.

"I now pronounce you man and wife," the minister said. "You may now kiss the bride, young man."

Abe looked away for fear that she would burst into tears right there in front of everyone, but then she had to look back because she didn't want to miss seeing Megan and Billy's first moments as husband and wife. Billy took Megan into his arms and kissed her. He whispered something in her ear and kissed her again. Then the bride and groom turned around and faced their guests, smiling brilliantly.

Tears were spilling down Abe's cheek by the time Billy and Megan walked back down the aisle. She would have forgotten when she was supposed to follow behind them had it not been for Jack confidently the lead. "It's our turn," he said, slipping his arm around her elbow. She let him lead the way, her heart pounding because he was so close. They walked down the aisle together, arm and arm. The guests were smiling at them and the photographer was madly snapping pictures, but all Abe could think about was Jack holding onto her arm and leading her to the door. His touch was firm but gentle. He was relaxed and confident and handsome, and he was with her. The knowledge that he was by her side warmed her to the center of her being.

They stood next to each other in the receiving line as the guests filed by to shake hands and offer congratulations to the bride and groom. Abe stood next to Jack, smiling at everyone and agreeing with them—yes, it was the most beautiful wedding she'd ever seen.

Chapter Thirteen

"Quit calling me Megan Meegen!"

"I'm sorry," Abe said. "I couldn't resist. But it is your name now, you know."

"I know that! Don't you think I know that?" Abe smiled so sweetly at the bride that all Megan could do was give her one more angry glare. "Brat," she said. "If I wasn't in this wedding gown, I'd slap you silly." Then she pinched Abe with her perfectly manicured hand.

"Ouch!"

"That's what you get and there's plenty more where that came from!"

The reception was in full swing from the moment Billy and Megan triumphantly swept into the room. Abe was seated at a long table next to the happy bride, Jack was sitting next to her on the other side—a seating arrangement that was perfect as far as Abe was concerned.

The band was playing after-dinner music but there was the sense that the tempo was becoming faster with each new song. The food was delicious and the celebration was going along as wonderfully as Megan hoped it would. Jack's hand rested lightly on Abe's back and he leaned in close. "I know," he said. "It's fun teasing the bride about her new name, isn't it?"

"Stop it," Megan said. "If I've said it once, I've said it a thousand times. Revenge will be mine."

"Yeah, yeah," Abe said. "You're in luck, I'm all worn out from teasing you now so I guess I'll stop, but only because it's your wedding day. Otherwise, I wouldn't hold back."

"Thanks," Megan said. "You're all heart." Then she looked at Abe and smiled. "You know, Jack, Abigail really likes to dance."

"She does, does she?"

"Oh yes, and she can really cut a rug. I think she'd love to dance now."

"Do you think I should?" Abe said. "The last time there was dancing it didn't go so well. I don't want any horrible accidents to happen."

"I think it's safe," Megan said. "There aren't any swimming pools here and the wedding cake is still safely in the kitchen."

"Ha, ha," Abe said, faking a punch to the bride.

"Let's go, Abigail," Jack said and offered her his hand.

Abe stood up and allowed Jack to lead her to the dance floor. "Okay," she said. "I'd love to dance. Maybe the band knows something by Refreshments in the Lobby."

They spent the next hour dancing. Abe enjoyed herself immensely, despite the dancers on the floor who invited her to join their conga line. Fortunately, her father was still forbidden to dance, although he didn't look happy about it. He was sitting at a round table with his wife looking longingly toward the dance floor. Occasionally, one of the bridesmaids would stop by his table and invite him to dance. Some even promised him that they'd see to it that he could dance with impunity.

"Don't even think about it," Abe said dancing past his table.

"Oh, come on," he moaned. "I've been practicing a new step and I wanted to try it out tonight."

"Nope. Sorry. Not happening tonight. Maybe next wedding."

"I'll give you ten bucks. Jack, help me out here. I wasn't that bad, was I?"

"You'd better make it twenty, sir," Jack said.

"Oh, all right," he said. "Twenty, but this is highway robbery!"

"Okay, you can dance," Abe said, taking the folded bill from her father and handing it to her mother for safekeeping. "But you better not start any trouble, you understand?"

"Me?" he said, and happily went out to the dance floor with a gaggle of laughing bridesmaids.

Mr. Gibson was dancing. This time it was a relatively tame step of hopping from foot to foot and jerking his head and shoulders to a beat all their own. Abe sighed and shook her head. The music was pounding and the snug-fitting gown she wore didn't afford her much room to dance. She decided not to be too ambitious for fear of ripping the dress up the side seams. But the music was so good and she felt so happy, that Abe threw caution to the wind and danced. Fortunately, the next hour was without incident. Then again, Wes and Susie were too busy huddled in a corner table to notice that others were dancing. The dancing made Abe feel wonderful, happy and relaxed despite her bopping father and her worries about her dress. Jack took her into his arms and they danced the night away.

It was a long time before they made their way back to the long table. Once there, they sipped wine. Neither one of them noticed Susie was behind them until they were almost there.

"Hi," she said, smiling. "You two looked great out there."

"Thanks, Susan," Jack said.

"Jack, can I speak to you for a moment?" Susie asked. Abe felt her mouth drop open and she wanted to tell Susie a resounding no, but Susie looked at her and smiled. "You don't mind, do you, Abigail? I promise I'll give him right back."

"No," Abe said, looking at Susie with deep suspicion. "Go right ahead."

Susie smiled at her again and led Jack away. They walked almost to the doorway, far enough from the noise of the band and the wedding guests but close enough for Abe to watch them. She sat by herself at the long table and sipped from her glass of white wine. Susie was holding onto Jack's arm and talking quickly, her face earnest. Abe wished she could hear what she was saying, but the room was too big and too noisy. All she knew was that Susie had Jack's undivided attention. They spoke for a full ten minutes before Susie gave him a quick peck on the cheek and handed him a white envelope. Abe watched as Jack walked back to the table.

"What was that all about?" Abe asked.

"Um . . . well, it's the oddest thing. Susan started talking about forgiveness and atonement and making things right. To tell you the truth, I didn't understand a lot of what she was saying, but I'm assuming she feels terrible about what happened. She gave me this." Jack held up the small white envelope.

"What is it?"

"It's two tickets to a concert."

"Tickets?"

"I didn't want to take them from her but she swore it was okay. She said she and Wes are going to Wilmington Beach for the day tomorrow and they can't use them."

"Tickets to what?"

"It's two tickets to see the Refreshments in the Lobby concert tomorrow."

"The Refreshments in the Lobby!" Abe's mouth dropped open once again. "Wow! You lucky duck! Those tickets have been sold out for weeks. How'd Susie get them?"

"She won them on a radio show. She said she was the tenth caller. She says that Refreshments in the Lobby is your favorite band and she wants us to have them. What do you say? Would you like to go with me?"

Abe couldn't believe her ears. "You have two tickets

to Refreshments in the Lobby and you want to know if I want to go?"

"Do you?"

"YES!"

Jack laughed. "Great. It'll be fun. You'll be finished with your maid-of-honor duties after tonight, right?"

"I sure hope so."

Abe could see Susie over Jack's shoulder. She was standing next to Wes and they were both grinning back at her and giving her a thumbs up.

"Oh, wow," Abe said, smiling back at them. "I'm going to see the Refreshments in the Lobby!"

Just then Abe felt a hand slip on her shoulder. She looked behind her and saw that the bride and groom were standing behind her.

"Did I hear what I think I heard?" Megan asked, with a giggle. "Are you going to see Refreshments in the Lobby?"

"Yes!" Abe said, almost shouting. "Can you believe it?"

"Hmm," Megan says. "If I didn't know better, I'd swear that this sounds almost like a date?"

"I guess it kind of is like a date," Abe said.

"So then," Megan said. "You and Jack have a date tomorrow, huh?"

"Uh-oh," Jack groaned. "Not again! Can't you two stop playing matchmaker long enough to cut the wedding cake?"

Megan and Billy grinned at each other knowingly. "This is perfect," Megan said. "Looks like our evil plan worked."

"I know," Billy agreed. "They fell right into our trap, didn't they?"

"I told you revenge would be mine," Megan said, her eyes glinting with mischief.

"And it's true what they say," Billy added. "Revenge IS sweet."

"Revenge?" Jack asked. "Revenge for what? What are you two talking about?"

"Yeah," Abe said. "You guys keep talking about revenge but you never actually get around to doing something about it."

"Oh?" Megan said. "Is that what you think?"

"Yep. That's what I think all right."

"But what you don't know is that I've been plotting my revenge for quite some time. In fact, my plan for revenge was so well executed, you still don't know what it is."

"And it was a brilliant plan," Billy added.

"Thank you, husband. It was brilliant, wasn't it?"

"And devious."

"That too."

"That's what I love about you."

"What are you talking about?" Jack asked, looking at them as if they'd both lost their minds.

"Oh, my goodness, Jack," Megan said. "Where are my manners? You know, with all the confusion of the past few weeks, I never properly introduced you two to each other. Did I, Billy?"

"No. You didn't, Megan, and that's just rude."

"You're right. It was rude of me, wasn't it? Well, I intend to change that right this very minute."

"That's okay, Megan," Jack said, twirling his finger

around his ear and looking at Abe with an alarmed expression on his face. "Abigail and I've already met."

"I know," Megan said. "But this is the South, after all, and you two were never formally introduced, were you?"

"Okay," Jack said, amused. "But I already know all I need to know about Abigail and I like what I see."

"Great," Megan said. "Jack, this is Abigail. Abigail Melinda Gibson, as a matter of fact."

"It's nice to meet you, Abigail Melinda Gibson." Jack seized Abe's hand and shook it warmly.

"Hi, there," she said, shaking his hand vigorously. "Nice to meet you too."

"But no one calls you Abigail though, do they?" Billy said, wrinkling his nose distastefully. "That's not the name you go by. In fact, Jack, the truth is Abigail hates to be called Abigail."

"Really?" Jack said looking at Abe curiously.

"That's right," Megan said. "Her given name's Abigail, but no one calls her that except for her grandma. But you see . . . well, my mother is rather formal, especially when it comes to my wedding."

"Yep," Billy chimed. "She's a formal lady all right. She's so formal, she asked the maid of honor at her youngest daughter's wedding to go by her given name. Can you imagine?"

Jack looked unimpressed. "It's true," Abe said and shrugged. "I hate the name Abigail. I only agreed to go along with being called Abigail because Mrs. Randal wanted me to. She also made Susie go by Susan."

Abe noticed that Jack looked baffled. "So," he said. "I'll start calling you Abbie right away. Not a problem."

"Nope," Megan said, hardly able to hide her delight. "She doesn't like to be called Abbie either. She much prefers to be called something else."

"What's that?" Jack asked.

"Just call me Abe," Abe said and was surprised to see Jack's mouth drop open and his eyes grow wide but before she could find out why, Billy was talking, or at least trying to. He was laughing so hard, she could barely understand him.

"Abe," he roared. "I never properly introduced you to my friend."

"I met your friend!" Abe laughed. "His name is Jack!"

"Jack what?" Megan asked, gleefully.

Abe looked at Jack, totally confused. "I don't know," she said, cocking her head to the side. "Come to think of it, I never did catch your last name."

But Jack was shaking his head and at the same time shaking Billy's hand.

"You did it," he said. "You got me. I admit it, this was the perfect revenge. I'll never tease Megan about her name again."

"Why not?" Abe said. She was starting to wonder if she was the only one among them who hadn't lost their mind.

"Abe," Megan said, beaming in evil joy. "I'd like you to meet my good friend, Jack. Jack LINCOLN."

Chapter Fourteen

SUNDAY, JUNE 24

$\mathbf{A}$be ran the hairbrush through her hair one last time. She looked in the mirror and couldn't help but smile. The butterflies that were fluttering softly since she woke up that morning were now going at full force, only now she didn't mind. Jack would be there any minute and she couldn't wait.

Just then, she heard the sound of the front door swing open. He was here! Abe gasped when she realized that the voices she heard was that of Jack and her father, who'd clearly escaped from her mother's watchful eye. She sprung from her room as if powered by a turbo. If she didn't get down the steps quickly, there was no telling what her father would do to him! Abe took the steps two at a time even though she suspected she sounded like a buffalo coming down the steps. She rushed into the living room, hoping against hope that her father didn't have Jack backed into a corner . . . or possibly even in a chokehold. Instead she found Jack sitting calmly in a chair across from her parents, a glass of iced tea in his hand.

"Hi, Abe," her father said when she galloped into the room. "I bumped into your friend outside. He's been telling me about his job at IBM."

Abe gave a panicked look to her mother. "How long have you been here?" she asked Jack warily, ignoring her father.

"Not long, maybe fifteen minutes. Traffic was light so I'm a little early."

Abe audibly gasped and quickly moved between him and her father. "Gotta go, folks," she said, taking the glass from Jack's hand and setting it down on the table. She then firmly took hold of his elbow and pulled him up from the chair.

"Walk out slowly," she whispered. "Don't make any sudden moves. I'll cover you for you as long as I can. Try to get to the car."

"What's the hurry, kids?" Abe's father asked. "The concert doesn't start for another two hours?"

Abe looked at her father incredulously. There was something very odd about him and again she looked toward her mother. Why, if she didn't know any better, she could swear he was being . . . friendly. "Are you okay, Dad?" she asked, genuinely concerned.

"I'm fine," he said. "But I'm a little worried about you, cupcake. Your mother just gave this young man that glass of iced tea, and you come in and snatch it clean out of his hand. Is that any way to treat your company?"

"Um . . . no?" Abe again looked at her mother questioningly. But Mrs. Gibson was as confused as Abe and only shrugged her shoulders.

"Sit down, Abe," her father said. "Certainly you have a few minutes to spare so that this young man can drink his iced tea. You'll have plenty of time to get to the concert. Now, Jack, tell me more about IBM. How long did you say you'd been working for them?"

Jack sat down again, somewhat confused himself, and launched into a conversation with Abe's father, as if it were a perfectly safe thing to do—as if any moment might not be his last.

Abe fleetingly wondered if her father was laying a trap for Jack, but if that was so, it wasn't the sort of thing he'd ever done before. No, she decided, her father was not good at playing possum. He was more the scary-guy type, the glaring and muttering under his breath kind. Abe sat on the edge of the sofa next to her father, poised to strike should her father make any sudden moves, while he and Jack discussed their respective jobs.

"Come back again, Jack," Abe's father said when they finally stood up to leave. "I've enjoyed talking with you."

"Thank you, sir," Jack said. "I've enjoyed talking with you too."

The two then shook hands which made Abe jump. "Hey!" she said to her father. "Watch it!"

"What?" he said, surprised. "What's gotten into you, Abe? You're awfully jumpy today."

"Me?" she gasped. "You're the one who's acting funny!"

"Okay then," Jack said, looking at Abe as if she were crazy. "We'd better go. I think."

He led Abe out the front door after saying another round of good-byes. "Your parents are nice," he told her when they finally made their escape.

"I don't think those were my parents," Abe said, frowning. "Well, at least that wasn't my dad. He sure looked like my dad though. He didn't threaten you, did he?"

"No," Jack said. "He was a nice guy. I like him."

"That doesn't sound at all like my dad. I'm starting to think my real dad was kidnapped and replaced by a space alien."

"If you say so," Jack said, smiling down at her.

Abe instantly forgot all about her father's possible abduction and turned her attention to the evening ahead. Now it was time to go to the concert. Jack led her to his car and opened the door for her. It was a practical, four-door, dark blue Honda. Not too old, not too new. It was perfect. Abe smiled and climbed inside. "Ready?" he said and she squinted into his face, the sunshine washing over them.

"Yes."

"I'm not," he said once he was behind the wheel. "I want to do this first," he said and leaned over her. He kissed her. Then he kissed her again. And again. Kisses that were delicious and warm and incredibly soft. He kissed her in a way she'd never been kissed. "Now I'm ready," he whispered after a gloriously long time.

They made it to the concert just in time. The traffic was heavy near the stadium, but they didn't mind. Every light and every stop was another opportunity to steal a kiss.

Once inside, they found their seats, which were surprisingly good. Jack and Abe spent the next few hours cheering and stomping their feet to the music and kissing each other when they could do so discreetly. The band was everything Abe hoped. Refreshments in the Lobby live and in person was better than she could have imagined. They played her old favorites along with some new music that hadn't been released yet but was as good, if not better, than anything they'd ever done before. Jack enjoyed the music too. Before long, they were dancing in the aisle. Naturally, Abe befriended all the people around them and by the end of the concert, their whole row was shouting and dancing and singing along together.

But amidst all the commotion, there were moments when nothing was said between Abe and Jack. Moments when they stared into each other's eyes and everything around them disappeared. These were the sweetest moments of the evening. A look or a soft touch of his hand was all that was necessary to make the butterflies return again and Abe would feel her knees go weak and her heart pound. It was wonderful.

She hated to see the night end. But all concerts come to an end, and eventually they found themselves saying good-bye to their newfound friends. They held hands as they made their way out of the crowded stadium to

Jack's car. It took a while, but they finally were able to get through the snarl of traffic and found a '50s-style diner which Abe had never been to. Jack said he'd been there before but it was a long time ago. It was one of those long, bullet-shaped, silver constructions with windows along all the walls and gleaming stainless steel everywhere.

Their waitress was dressed in uniform. It was a pink, full-skirted dress trimmed in black piping with a lace collar and a frilly white apron. Her hair was done in a beehive bun and she wore bright pink lipstick, too much blush and a nametag that said SALLY JANE.

"Sit anywhere you want, sugar," she said in a deep, southern drawl. "I'll be with you in two shakes of a lamb's tail."

They found a booth, and Jack slid in next to Abe. True to her promise, Sally Jane arrived at their table quickly. They ordered cheeseburgers and french fries and milkshakes. It was the sort of food Abe seldom allowed herself, but given the ambiance of the restaurant, she couldn't wait to dig in. "I don't usually eat this way," Jack said, echoing her thoughts.

"Me either. I'm more of a pasta and salad kind of gal, but this is great."

"I'm more of a beer and barbecue kind of guy."

He was sitting close, and Abe wished that the night would last forever. They hardly spoke as they waited for the food, preferring instead to just look at each other and smile.

"Did you have a good time?" Jack asked. His voice was low and husky and he was looking into her eyes.

"Yes," she said, her own voice was low as well. "Did you?"

"Yes," he said.

And then he kissed her and she melted into his arms. She could feel his heart pounding and butterflies in her stomach. She was crazy about him.

"Now y'all go right ahead with your smooching," the waitress said, banging down the tall silver tumblers that held the milkshakes. "Don't let me bother y'all none. I was young once. I remember it well." She set down two milkshake glasses and beamed an ear-to-ear smile at them.

Abe blushed and Jack smiled. "Sorry," he said to Sally Jane.

"Now don't you apologize," she said. "You two are the cutest things I've seen all night long."

Abe and Jack looked at each other and blushed and then laughed. They suspected Sally Jane was right—they did look cute together.

"We better behave ourselves," he said after the waitress left them alone to sip on the thick milkshakes.

"Agreed," Abe said, blushing again. "Do you think Megan and Billy are in their hotel yet?"

"Probably. I don't think it's a long flight to the Bahamas. What time did they leave this morning?"

"About noon, I think. Megan wouldn't tell me what hotel they stayed at last night."

"Billy wouldn't say either. I think they were afraid we'd crash in on them. And we would have too. Alex and Nathan were going to send them a pizza."

"I heard they tried to get Megan's dad to tell them

where they were but he wouldn't budge. Taylor and Chandler weren't going to take it that far. They were just going to take turns calling their room and saying, 'so, what are you doing?' "

"Brats."

"They are. I told Megan I'd never do anything like that to her."

"Really?"

"Heck no. I was lying through my teeth."

"Did she believe you?"

"Not for a second. I don't think I would have been able to pass up the opportunity to torture her. Not a lot though. Just a little. She is my best friend, after all. But it might have been fun to booby trap their room."

"Yeah. Some itching powder in the bed maybe. We have to get back at them for all those blind dates they tried to set us up on."

"I know! I hate when they do that!"

He looked at her and smiled slyly. "Do you really? Still?"

She smiled back. "No," she said. "Not so much anymore. I've had a good time on our date. Although, technically, it wasn't a blind date because we'd already met."

"I had a good time too. It's been an interesting six days."

"Six days?" Abe said, tipping her head to the side. "It hasn't been six days. I know it doesn't seem like it, but this is only our first date."

"True enough. This is our first actual date, but I've

been keeping count. So far, it's been six days that we've seen each other."

"What do you mean?"

"I met you at the pizza parlor; that was the first day. Then there was the barbecue. That was day two."

"Yes. I made quite a splash that night, didn't I?"

"Yes, you did, and I've never seen anyone more beautiful." His eyes were shining, and Abe's heart skipped a beat.

"The wedding shower was day three," she said.

"Yes. That meeting was supposed to have led to our first date, but things didn't go the way I'd hoped they would."

"I remember," Abe said. She'd all but forgotten about Jack leaving with Susie.

"The rehearsal dinner was on day four," he continued. "And the wedding was five, and today . . . today is the sixth day I've seen you."

"I can't believe you've been keeping count."

"Yes. I didn't mean to, but I realized from the first day that I couldn't stand it when I wasn't with you, so I started counting. So far, it's been six days."

"Six days in June. You're right. I wasn't keeping count, but I couldn't wait to see you either."

"I was," he said and kissed her again. It was so sweet and wonderful, Abe felt like crying. Jack looked up cautiously, hoping Sally Jane wasn't watching. "I think Billy and Megan finally got it right," he whispered. "Even if my last name is Lincoln and your first name is Abe."

"They'd planned it all along," she said in amazement. "The way Megan insisted that everyone call me Abigail. I bet her mother didn't care one bit what everyone called me. She may even have been in on it with Megan!"

"I can't believe no one spilled the beans! Or slipped."

"You're right!" Abe said. "It was a conspiracy!"

"I think so too," Jack said. "But it was just too perfect a setup not to try it. They just had to do it."

"Yeah, now they're all hoping that you and I will fall in love and get married. Then I'll be Mrs. Abe Lincoln." She grimaced when she said it. "I didn't think anything could be as bad as Megan Meegan."

"I don't know," he said with a grin. "You could always go back to being Abigail again. Or you could keep your maiden name after we're married."

"What fun is that?" Abe said laughing. "Besides, it would ruin Billy and Megan's plan. I guess I'm just going to have to get used to being named Abe Lincoln."

"It's settled then," he said. "You're going to have to fall in love with me now."

"And you have to fall in love with me—if only for the humor value."

"It would be too good to pass it up, wouldn't it? I hope you don't mind marrying me."

"Not at all, but only if you promise not to tease me about my new name."

"Deal. I'm sure Megan and Billy will handle that end of things. Me, I like your new name. Abe Lincoln has a nice ring to it." He kissed her again, not caring that it was still only their first date and that Sally Jane was smiling at them from the kitchen.